"*Through Three Rooms* is an entertaining country house mystery novella from the early twentieth century, in which the great Norwegian detective Asbjørn Krag tries to uncover the secrets of a rich and eccentric old man who has suddenly begun to fear for his life. The pace is fast and the story an enjoyable example of the traditional murder mystery."

— *Martin Edwards, novelist and author of The Life of Crime*

"*Through Three Rooms* is a brisk, pacey and thoroughly entertaining page-turner by one of crime fiction's unsung heroes. It's a good old-fashioned thriller that benefits immeasurably from a concise, skilful translation, and is well worth rediscovering."

— *Tom Mead, author of Death and the Conjuror*

"Like the expert marksmanship displayed in this story, Riverton shows excellent aim in picking off our (genre-trained) assumptions about the mystery enclosed. Fortunately police detective Asbjørn Krag, Norway's answer to Sherlock Holmes, is not so dazzled by the 'inexplicable and the mysterious' in this country house murder mystery."

— *Kate Jackson, author of*
How to Survive a Classic Crime Novel (2023)
and Crossexamining Crime blog (www.crossexaminingcrime.com)

THROUGH THREE ROOMS

SVEN ELVESTAD

KABATY PRESS
Published by Kabaty Press, Warsaw
www.kabatypress.com

NORLA
Norwegian
Literature Abroad

This translation has been published with the financial support of
NORLA (Norwegian Literature Abroad)

ISBN: 978-83-966166-2-3 (Paperback)
      978-83-966166-3-0 (Hardcover)
      978-83-966166-4-7 (ePub)
      978-83-966166-5-4 (PDF)

TABLE OF CONTENTS

The Man with a Thousand Irons in the Fire

We might say that Norwegian crime fiction started in the year 1821, with the publication of a short psychological thriller, *Den gale Christian* ('Christian the Madman') by Mauritz Christopher Hansen (1794–1842). Hansen wrote several stories that herald the development of crime and detective fiction and certainly his 100 page novel *Mordet paa Maskinbygger Roolfsen* ('The Murder of Engineer Roolfsen) – published around the New Year in 1840, thus antedating Poe's *The Murders in the Rue Morgue* by fifteen months – comes impressively close to being a proper detective story in the modern sense, with a surprise solution, a policeman investigating and even a sort of Agatha Christie type of fair misdirection in the title. But this was at a time when the reading public of Norway consisted of just a few thousand people, and even fewer had the money to buy books. Hansen's most famous pupil was in fact the dramatist Henrik Ibsen who learned from him the retrospective technique he employs in his contemporary plays, the unravelling of secrets of the past.

So despite Mauritz Hansen's achievement, the history of Norwegian crime fiction properly begins in 1897, with the publication of *Karl Monks Oplevelser* ('The Adventures of Karl Monk'). By then, the works of the great pioneers of the genre, such as Gaboriau, Collins, Fergus Hume and Conan Doyle, had been translated and the detective story had quickly become immensely popular, especially with the rapidly increasing middle classes. The working-class reading audience had multiplied, paving the way for cheap fiction of the Penny Dreadful/Dime Novel kind, much of it marginally crime fiction. It was a Norway very different from the one that Mauritz Hansen knew, a modern world of steam engines, automobiles, telephones and bicycles, and with a capital that had speedily grown into a small metropolis, complete with an underworld.

Karl Monk, a chief of police turned private investigator, was created by Naval officer Christian Sparre (1859–1940), under the pseudonym of Fredrik Viller (this was the start of a long tradition of using aliases – often English-sounding – for crime writing in Norway). Monk is described as "the complete opposite to Sherlock Holmes", and true, he is a more emotional character: he resigned from his police job for the love of a woman who was a suspect in a case. But like everybody else at the time, Viller/Sparre found it difficult to escape from the shadow of the Master of Baker Street.

So did at first Stein Riverton alias Sven Elvestad (1884–1934), journalist and sybarite *extraordinaire* who made his debut some years later than Sparre. He was born in Fredrikshald (present Halden) and his father was a ship's captain who perished at sea, leaving his sixteen-year-old son to support his mother and two siblings. Luckily young Sven (he was in fact baptized Kristofer Elvestad Svendsen) was something of a child prodigy; he had started writing for newspapers at fourteen and published a couple of detective stories at the tender age of 17. The crime writing career started in earnest two years later, in 1904, after he had moved to Norway's capital Kristiania and gained employment in a newspaper there. His first efforts were published anonymously as newspaper serials, what the French called *feuilletons*. But when two of the stories were collected in book form in 1907, they were signed "Stein Riverton". A friend had suggested the *nom-de-guerre*, a strong Norwegian first name (it means "rock") combined with an English translation of the name Elvestad.

Elvestad created his own private detective Asbjørn Krag, who like Monk was also a former police investigator and started out in the tradition of Holmes; he is mysterious, romantic, infallible, excentric and aristocratic. He is "somewhere in his thirties" (but in the first story we are told that he served in the Kristiania (Oslo) CID from 1873 to 1893) and is of course tall and athletic, "with a high, bald forehead". But he wears a pince-nez and a moustache, which makes him look rather like Captain Dreyfus (he is also said to resemble an English boxer, whatever that means) and over the years he develops a rather split personality; on the one hand he is a full-blooded action hero, always on the track of some master criminal, quick to brandish guns and command the railway's "latest steel giant" in order to pursue the villains; on the other – in Elvestad's best novels – he is a patient, quiet but unrelenting tracker of the truth, willing to spend unlimited time in order for the villain to break down, rather similar to Porfiry Petrovich in *Crime and Punishment* by Dostoyevsky, who was an important inspiration to Elvestad, along with Doyle and Poe.

Although Sparre continued to publish new books sporadically over the next couple of decades, he and others of the time were overshadowed by Elvestad, who, it can be claimed, *was* the first golden age of Norwegian crime fiction. His most serious rival was Øvre Richter Frich (1872–1945) who mainly wrote adventure and science fiction novels rather than crime, starring Dr Jonas Fjeld, an ancestor of Bulldog Drummond and James Bond. And Elvestad's influence lasted a long time; his police detective Knut Gribb, created in 1908 for a Dime Novel – or rather Nickel Weekly – series to compete with Nick Carter who had then made his entry into Scandinavia, lived to be a hundred in magazines and books and, finally, a popular radio drama series. Elvestad wrote the first 28 issues all of which he later republished as Asbjørn Krag novels, being always on the lookout for the easy buck. Over the years more than 80 writers contributed to the Knut Gribb saga, and if Gribb doesn't top the list in the number of adventures (about 1,600 against Sexton Blake's nearly 4,000) he has certainly had the longest life.

Stein Riverton (the alias was used only in Norway and Sweden, he was Sven Elvestad elsewhere) was immensely prolific. He was, to borrow the title of one of his novels, the proverbial *Manden med tusen jern i ilden* (1925, 'The Man with a Thousand Irons in the Fire'). Even while producing every week for seven months a complete Knut Gribb novelet, he continued to write newspaper serials about Asbjørn Krag and started on his allegedly greatest novel *The Iron Chariot*, as well as pursued his calling as a journalist. In all, he published 90 titles. Only a small handful of his crime fiction was short stories, the rest varied from novelet up to full length novels. At a certain time the demand was so great that Elvestad set his associate Christian Haugen – shades of Alexandre Dumas! – to write four Riverton novels (not the present one).

And his popularity didn't stop at the borders; with *The Iron Chariot* he made his breakthrough internationally and during the years 1910 to 1925 he reigned supreme as King of Crime in northern Europe; he had books published in 17 languages, including Hungarian, Spanish and Serbo-Croat, and he had a particularly large following in Sweden and Germany. In fact, there were more titles published by him in those countries than in his native Norway. Very few were translated into English, though. *Mannen som ville plyndre Kristiania* (1915) was published as *The Man Who Plundered the City* in the U.S.A in 1924, and *Montrose* as *The Mystery of the Abbé Montrose* (1917) in U.K. in the same year (with the name Asbjørn Krag anglicised to Osborne Crag!). No new translation followed *Fænomenet Robert Robertsson* (1925) which was published both in the U.K. and the

U.S.A. in 1930 as *The Case of Robert Robertsson*, despite the fact that it received high praise by no lesser authority than Dashiell Hammett ("… easily one of the season's best … here is work for translators.").

The books were highly topical; they mirrored the advances of the times and spanned all layers of society from the alluring *demi-monde* of the restaurants to the mean streets of crime and squalor; they caught the pulse of their time. Four years before the Bonnot gang created a sensation in France by using automobiles to commit crimes Elvestad had villains doing the same. (Incidentally, Elvestad was in France at the time of the Bonnot affair and got arrested as a suspect, but that's another story.) He felt that the detective story was the perfect sort of fiction for the modern age of speed and technical innovation, "the age of the screaming disharmonies". He was himself a part of this rush; most of the novels were written for magazine and newspaper serial publication and then appeared in book form, breezily composed at restaurant tables and in hotel rooms while the author pursued the noisy "moveable feast" that he craved, often with the office boy waiting at his side to take the next chapter to the printer. In consequence, too many of them are loosely plotted and haphazardly constructed. But Elvestad was never less than a brilliant stylist – there is an echo of the early Hamsun in his work – and even in his less successful stories there are gems of description, where time and place come wondrously alive.

And a dozen or so of his books are truly great. A couple

of them belong arguably among the best crime novels ever written, tales of haunting psychological terror: *Jernvognen* (1909, 'The Iron Chariot'), a murder mystery set in the pale Nordic summer, anticipates by 17 years the trick that Agatha Christie would use in *The Murder of Roger Ackroyd*. (Elvestad may have been inspired by Anton Chekhov's *Death in the Forest*, and Christie may have been inspired by suggestions from both her brother-in-law and Lord Mountbatten, as she claimed. But, for what it is worth, it seems to be an established fact that a British magazine ran *The Iron Chariot* as a serial in the early '20s.) And *Morderen fra mørket* (1913, 'The Murderer from the Dark'), based on a real life unsolved Swedish murder case, has a similarly surprising denouement and an intensely observed feeling of nature and light – or darkness as it were: in contrast to *Jernvognen* it is set in the bleakest part of winter.

The first edition of *Morderen fra mørket* was signed Sven Elvestad and the detective has no name. This shows that its author kept it in special high regard. Riverton was the crime writer. Sven Elvestad was the journalist, the essayist and the author of a few ambitious short stories and novels. However the novels, such as *De fortaptes hus* (1912, 'The House of the Lost') and *Færgestedet* (1928, 'The Ferry Landing') often have a murder at their centre.

Among his best crime works is also the present novel, first published as a newspaper serial in 1907 to '08 as *Gjennem de tre Værelser. Af Kristiania-Detektiven Asbjørn Krags Oplevelser* and in book form in 1915, under the title

Dødens finger ('The Finger of Death' – the explanation for which is not given in the story), it became one of his best sellers. Another Krag novel worth noting in addition to those mentioned above is *Fjærdemand* (1921, 'The Fourth Man') and late non-Krag titles such as *Hvorledes dr Wrangel kom* (1927, 'How Dr Wrangel Arrived'), *Djevelen kjeder sig* (1929, 'The Devil Is Bored') and his final *homage* to the city of Oslo/Kristiania, *Hertuginnen av Speilsalen* (1931, 'The Grand Duchess of the Hall of Mirrors' – Speilsalen remains an attraction of the Grand Hotel).

Elvestad became an international celebrity. A distinct appearance, gigantic in stature, extremely myopic eyes and a face that betrayed his passion for food and drink and tobacco, made him popular with painters and cartoonists. In one of his books, he describes a man who sits still and *drinks* his chair to pieces — he might have been describing himself. His lifestyle was in fact legendary. In his later years he would start off the day with a bottle of cognac and then follow up with about 25 pints of wine and 120 cigarettes. This was especially when he was abroad – which he was a lot of the time, especially in Sweden, Germany, and Italy. There are a huge number of fantastic stories about his adventures in foreign lands, for instance – true or not? – such as the one told by a Swedish friend of how he travelled with Elvestad and a crowd of others through Germany, and everywhere they stopped presented a cheque of such value that no hotel or restaurant could exchange it. Italy became his regular haunt in later years; in his favourite town Positano he became a celebrity under the title of "il Professore". As a journalist he was capable of all kinds of stunts; he once spent an hour in the lion cage at the Zoo while reading a newspaper to win a bet; he suffered through an experiment at sea with a newly invented lifebuoy; he was one of the first foreign reporters to interview the rising leading figure of the German Nazi Party, Adolf Hitler, who scared him stiff. But in his best work – characteristically, one of the novels he published under his own name in Norway, is called *Angsten* (1911, 'The Anxiety') – the face of another man appears, a complex personality, deeply concerned with guilt and fear, the man who wrote prophetically about the rise of militarism and the possible abuse of technological progress long before World War I. Behind this face is also that of a closet homosexual. Although not unexperienced with women, he preferred his own sex, and how that was viewed upon at that time need hardly be deliberated upon.

He used to step out though when he was abroad, especial in the liberal southern Italy. That may be part of the reason (but hardly the only one), that in his later years he became an admirer of Mussolini and Fascism. He welcomed Vidkun Quisling and his National Socialist party in 1933 and although sceptical of some features of Nazi Germany he looked upon it with a certain approval, even when homosexuality was given as the grounds for a massacre by Röhm and his SD troops.

Was he an anti-semite? The evidence is at best contradictory. Was he a true fascist? When asked about this in an interview (in a Socialist newspaper!) his answer is: "It is *I* that am a Fascist! I was a Fascist already while Mussolini was still a Socialist agitator and Hitler went about grumbling because he was told to paint the boardings vertically and he wanted to paint them horizontally."

It is somehow hard to picture Elvestad, all 120 eccentric kilos of him and the bluest nose north of the Alps, marching along with a rank of booted Blackshirts. And anyway, the matter never came to the test.

On the 18 December 1934, three months after his 50th birthday, he prepared to go on board a ship bound for Palestine. He checked in at a local hotel – the ship would sail in the evening – and here he became very pleasantly acquainted with a fellow-traveller who was incidentally a Jewish rabbi. But the years of burning his candle at both hands and the middle too, finally took their toll on his heart. When his young secretary and partner who had been out on an errand came back, he found Elvestad dead. (Not really in their room but in the nearby toilet. Which hasn't prevented the hotel from keeping up the pleasant superstition that the room is haunted.)

Ironically, he had already supplied his colleagues of the press with the perfect headline: One of his books is called *Døden tar ind på hotellet* ('Death Checks Into the Hotel').

He left a considerable debt, mainly to his publishers. This was paid off with the publication of a ten-volume set of his Riverton novels. Although reprints of his books have been few and far between in the years since, his alias has been kept green by the crime writers of Norway who in 1972 started the Riverton Club, a society for the cultivation and improvement of crime fiction, like the Crime Writers' Association in the U.K. and The Mystery Writers of America. It gives out an annual award for the best Norwegian work of crime fiction, called popularly the Riverton Prize. And since Krag had two golden duelling pistols, the trophy naturally is a gun with a gilded handle. It used to be a Nagant, now it's a Smith & Wesson. A special honorary Riverton prize is reserved for distinguished service to Norwegian crime fiction. There is also an honorary international Riverton prize which is given out occasionally, among its recipients are PD James, Maj Sjöwall and Henning Mankell.

And although there are hardly more than a couple of Riverton books in print in the original language at any time these days, almost a score can be found as audiobooks, produced in the last few years. The voice on most of them I'm honoured to say is mine.

— *Nils Nordberg*

CHAPTER 1

The Doctor's Tale

One winter evening some three years ago, Asbjørn Krag was sitting by the fireplace in his apartment, leafing through a huge folder of documents he had just received from one of his clients. The lamp cast a sharp light on the papers, which were many and various—yellowed letters, diverse accounts, numerous telegrams. Suddenly the detective gave a start: a ring at the doorbell.

Krag put down the papers. A man's voice was audible in the hall.

Surmising that the new arrival was a client, the detective quickly stood up, dimmed and then doused the lamp. Next, he turned a knob, and a powerful beam of electric light streamed at once from a green lamp, straight at the door—just as it opened and a gentleman stepped into the room.

A ruddy-faced, somewhat portly middle-aged gentleman in gold-rimmed spectacles, he stopped in surprise on the threshold, half-blinded by the harsh light. At first, he failed to see Asbjørn Krag, who stood over in the gloom behind the lamp.

Stepping forward with a laugh, Krag seized the new-comer's hand and shook it warmly.

"Do shut the door, old friend, you're letting a tremendous blast of cold air into my study."

The gentleman in the gold-rimmed spectacles quickly closed the door.

"I didn't see you at first, my dear Krag," he said. "I say, that's a damned powerful floodlight you have there."

Krag laughed again.

"I like to examine my clients' faces when they first come to visit me," he answered. "Ever since I was fooled by a man in a false beard one winter evening five years ago, I have always ensured that I have plenty of light in the vicinity. But do sit down and let's have a proper chat. How delightful of you to visit me in my solitude. It has been a long time since we last saw one another."

The gentleman in the gold-rimmed spectacles was pressed into an armchair and Asbjørn Krag seated himself comfortably opposite. The detective picked up the folder he had been leafing through and tossed the papers indifferently upon a table.

"Dull drudgery," he muttered. "There's no end to the business fraud I'm obliged to deal with in these wicked, wicked times. But now we shall set all that aside. Here, have a Havana cigar—the best the city has to offer."

The unknown gentleman lit a cigar.

"So you recognized me at once," he said. "I had not expected that."

"How could I fail to recognize my old schoolfriend, Karl Rasch?" Krag answered. "It may be many years since we last met, but I can always rely on my policeman's eye, you know. So you're a doctor now?"

"Yes, I am. I have a practice down south, in Smaalenene County." He glanced at the documents on the table and asked, hesitantly but with interest: "Are you very busy with that case?"

"A mere bagatelle. Don't trouble yourself about it in the slightest. I have plenty of time."

"Is there any chance that you could defer it for a few days?"

Asbjørn Krag's interest was piqued. He stood up.

"Ah, so you are seeking my assistance?"

"Yes," answered the doctor. "Frankly, I need your help— not so much for myself as for a patient. An old gentleman who is about to get married."

"A dread ailment indeed," Krag murmured playfully.

"This is no laughing matter," the doctor objected. "I have pondered it over the course of many sleepless nights but have been unable to find any solution."

"What do the police say?"

"The police must not be involved."

"Aha." Krag had grown interested. "I shall, of course, be delighted to take the case," he said. "But quickly now, tell me everything, first to last. I dislike prevarication."

The doctor looked at his watch.

"You must travel down there with me," he said. "The

night train south leaves in one hour and twenty minutes, so we shall have plenty of time for conversation."

"How many days should I expect to be away?" asked the detective.

"I don't know yet. Three or four, I'd say."

Asbjørn Krag rang for his manservant and issued the following instructions. "Holdall Number 2; a cab to the eastern railway station at 10.45 pm."

As the manservant was about to leave, Krag stopped him, seized by a thought. Turning to the doctor, he asked: "Dangerous?"

The doctor seemed unsure and did not reply.

"Good," said the detective. "Pack the little black box, Jens."

The manservant left, and Krag sat down. He chose the armchair closest to the fire, which burned red and restful.

"I am all ears," he said.

The doctor began his tale.

"Are you familiar with Kvamberg Manor? I see you are nodding. Of course—who does not know it? It is, after all, among the largest and best-known estates in the country. It has changed hands three times over the past fifteen years. Some five years ago, a rich Swedish-American arrived in the village. The owner of Kvamberg had just died in an accident—he fell out of a tower window—and his family then sold the farm to the Swedish-American, whose name is John Aakerholm. The new owner made certain changes at the manor, fitting out the rooms according to his own somewhat peculiar tastes. To start off with, he lived in fairly lavish style, giving parties and making many friends. The eccentric old gentleman—who spoke in a curious blend of Norwegian, Swedish and English, and had the air of an old general put out to pasture—was very well liked, and people were glad to meet at his hospitable home. But little by little, he seemed to tire of this social activity, eventually curtailing it altogether. In recent years, there has not been a single party at Kvamberg. However, he keeps company with a few good friends, with whom he enjoys a hand of cards of an evening, drinking with them in the town club and telling them stories. For he has always been a great storyteller, the old man—hardly surprising, given his life on the prairies and in the gold-mining districts, whose adventures and marvels would be hard to match.

"As his doctor, I have frequented his home a great deal. He fears nothing in the whole wide world and has looked death in the eye on many occasions; however, like so many other brave men he is something of a hypochondriac, so I was summoned at all hours of the day and night. Sometimes, I would stay overnight at the farm, and would then be given a room that lay as far away as possible from the old man's own bedroom. I did not pay much attention to this at first, but when I heard from the servants that the old man always slept alone at night and had strictly forbidden anyone from approaching his rooms, the whole business began to seem a little odd. To begin with, I thought it was just some foible of the old warhorse …"

Asbjørn Krag interrupted the doctor. "You said rooms. So are there several rooms that no one may enter?"

"In order to reach the old man's bedroom, one must pass through two rooms and three doors. During the daytime, no one is barred from the two ante-rooms. But once the clock has struck twelve and the old man has gone to bed, no one may enter any of the rooms. He himself locks them securely and he is the only one with a key."

"What floor are these rooms on?"

"The second. But to prevent anyone from entering his room through the window, he has installed a ledge encircled with barbed wire, which makes entry impossible."

"And there is no ingress to the old man's bedroom other than through the two rooms and the three doors?"

"No. His bedroom is at the end of that wing of the manor."

"Perhaps he hides his valuables in this room. Is he very wealthy?"

"Indeed he is, extremely so. But all his money is deposited with Norwegian and Swedish banks."

Krag sat by the fireplace, puffing away at his cigar. He pondered.

"Now we come to the truly remarkable part of the story," the doctor continued.

"And this remarkable part," Krag shot in, "begins with old Aakerholm's marriage plans, no doubt."

"Quite so. For now, I shall say nothing about the lady in question. You may see her for yourself when you arrive down there. But I do not like her. She comes from a middle-class family, is no longer quite young but is very pretty, a widow. She is known as 'the Silken Girl' owing to the expensive finery she favours. While he was still alive, her late husband—a timber merchant and grocer named Hjelm—took her frequently abroad with him. By small-town standards, she has lived an altogether luxurious life. When the estate was settled after Hjelm's death, there proved to be nothing left for the widow. She has since had some difficulty maintaining her extravagant ways and in the end, one cannot blame her for welcoming the haven of prosperity old Aakerholm is offering her at Kvamberg."

Asbjørn Krag nodded.

"A marriage of convenience, then."

"Precisely. Aakerholm is cool-headed enough to admit that love plays no part in the matter, on her side at least. Some three weeks ago, he informed me that a date for the wedding had been set in two months' time, in other words at Christmas. Late one afternoon a few days afterwards, I was summoned urgently to Kvamberg. The old squire had suddenly fallen ill, and this time he was genuinely sick —"

The doctor lit a fresh cigar and continued.

"I assure you, my dear Krag, that in all my years as a doctor I have never seen a man undergo so abrupt and dreadful a change. Handsome old Aakerholm with his calm, courageous eyes and vigorous bearing had become a trembling, timorous old man. When I arrived, he was lying on a sofa in one of the drawing rooms; his hair and beard had turned almost white and his eyes stared, hopeless and afraid, from a face that seemed ravaged by fear. I examined him immediately and found him in a state of great nervous agitation. I realized at once that whatever he had experienced, this turmoil alone could easily have killed him.

"I gave him a sedative and an hour later he was more or less his old self. I asked him what had happened, but he gave a brief, evasive answer: Nothing. I ordered him to bed and watched the old man stagger slowly and unsteadily through the two rooms and the three doors into his own bedroom. I made to follow him, but already on the threshold of the first room he turned to face me and sent me the most ferocious glare. I drew back hastily. Some days then passed and the old man became calmer, but had a somewhat thoughtful and brooding air about him. He had become quieter and more reserved. I visited him often and he liked me to stay with him for a long time —"

"Permit me a question," the detective broke in. "Had he abandoned his marriage plans at this point?"

"On the contrary. He became even more determined that the marriage should take place."

"Good. Do go on."

"One afternoon, perhaps a week later, something rather odd happened when I sat conversing with him. I was in an armchair sipping a glass of liqueur while the old man walked back and forth, puffing on a pipe of shag. Suddenly, something caught his attention, and he stood staring into the huge drawing-room mirror in mute, motionless terror.

Before I could stop him, he seized a heavy fruit bowl and hurled it at the mirror, whose green depths were entirely shattered into tiny pieces. I jumped up in alarm, shouting 'What in God's name are you doing, man!' But he stopped me, placed his two trembling hands upon my shoulders and replied: 'Nothing, nothing… leave me in peace. Go, doctor. I must be alone.' And I left."

Asbjørn Krag nodded thoughtfully.

"Could you see into the mirror yourself?" he asked the doctor.

"No," the doctor said. "I was ill-placed to do so. It was a great old-fashioned mirror of considerable value."

"Do you think the pieces have been preserved?"

"I believe so. They are probably lying on some rubbish heap."

"Have you spoken to the old man since?"

"Yes, several times. However, he has always steered the conversation away from the incident with the mirror. But then, yesterday afternoon, I was called urgently to Kvamberg once more and this time I found the old man in a state that was, if anything, worse than on the first occasion. He had returned from a stroll in the grounds of the manor quite out of his wits, scared to death. As I tended to him, I heard him whisper several times: 'Is he a devil or a man?' Today, I visited again: he was up and about and improved in all respects, although still most despondent. I asked what had happened to him on his walk, but received only the customary, evasive reply: Nothing, nothing…

"That was when I decided to come to you, Asbjørn Krag, and ask you to intervene. Did I do wrong?"

Krag looked at his watch and stood up.

"No," he said. "You did right. I am grateful that you came."

"But the old man knows nothing of my visit."

"Naturally."

"We can of course pass you off as a specialist in nervous diseases."

"Yes, or something else. We shall hit upon a solution. But now we must leave. The train departs in a matter of minutes."

The doctor asked hesitantly, "Do you believe some danger is brewing? A crime perhaps?"

"Indubitably."

Krag opened the door and called out to his manservant. "Don't forget to pack the little black box."

Turning to the doctor, he continued: "There is only one thing you have failed to tell me. Who sent you the urgent summons?"

"It was the son. The old man's adopted son, Bengt."

"Aha, so there is an adopted son too? I thought it unlikely that the old man was alone. I must hear more about him. But now let us leave and you can tell me about this Bengt Åkerholm along the way."

A moment later, the two gentlemen were driving through the streets of Kristiania to the eastern railway station. It was a freezing winter evening with light snowfall.

CHAPTER 2

THE MAN IN THE DARKNESS

Asbjørn Krag and the doctor had a compartment to themselves on the express train south.

They made themselves comfortable in the warm compartment and lit their cigars. The curtains were drawn across the windows and the sliding doors were closed.

"I am delighted I was able to persuade you to travel down there with me," the doctor said. "It was good of you, considering how very busy you are."

"Tremendously busy," Krag replied. "But whenever a case that I find particularly interesting presents itself, I put aside everything else I have in hand. And this case certainly does interest me. So, there is an adopted son then."

"Yes, somewhere between twenty-five and thirty years of age."

"Do you know anything about him?"

"Not a thing. He's a shipbroker in the neighbouring town, spends a great deal of his time at the club, and is said to be a clever little businessman. But I gather he displays no great talent in any particular direction."

"Nationality?"

"Swedish-American, like his father—who adopted him when he was seventeen or eighteen."

"Do you know why?"

"Merely because he was the son of an old friend of Aakerholm's who died in America, it seems. For despite his grumbling, Aakerholm is a good-hearted soul."

"And what does this fellow Bengt have to say about these peculiar incidents?"

"He says he cannot understand them."

"It is clear enough," Krag continued, "that old Aakerholm's experiences have left him in a state of the utmost terror. He has certainly seen something."

"He has become an old man in a matter of weeks," the doctor murmured. "I am convinced that there is danger brewing. He could die at any moment."

"So," the detective said, "it would seem reasonable to assume that someone stands to gain from the old man's death. Who could it be? Bengt?"

The doctor looked at Krag.

"The same thought occurred to me," he answered. "But I have been forced to dismiss it. I have no idea what might have happened to the old man, but whatever it was, it happened at Kvamberg or in the immediate vicinity of the manor. And in both cases, Bengt was absent. The first time, I alerted him myself by telephone. At the time, he was at his office in the nearby town and when he arrived there, he was completely taken aback—and genuinely so. I could tell by looking at him."

"Nonetheless, we cannot rule the man out quite yet," Krag objected. "If a crime is being planned, as I am inclined to believe, Bengt is the only person who will truly benefit from Aakerholm's death. As I understand it, he stands to inherit the old man's fortune. He is, of course, opposed to the old man's marriage plans."

"He is. But old Aakerholm has pointed out to him that his financial future is secure regardless of the marriage. The old man is that rich."

When Asbjørn Krag and the doctor disembarked at the little provincial station, Aakerholm's sleigh awaited them. They bundled themselves up in wolfskins then sped along the roads on smoothly gliding runners beneath the moonlit winter night. The cold nipped fiercely at their faces.

After a half-hour drive, they came in sight of the manor, which was set in magnificent grounds. Krag thought to himself that in summertime the manor must be quite buried beneath a mound of tree canopies.

As the sleigh turned off the road and swung in towards the great courtyard, the doctor rose up with a cry of surprise and ordered the driver to halt.

"Look there!" he shouted, pointing across the garden. Its depths were lit by flickering torches, in whose red glimmer human figures came and went.

The doctor leaned towards the driver and asked, "What is the meaning of this?"

"It's the master," replied the driver. "He's ordered the pavilion in the garden to be torn down."

The detective looked at the driver, who was smiling, and understood the import of that smile.

"Let us go over," he said. They both alighted and walked towards the torches as quickly as the deep snow permitted.

When they got there, Asbjørn Krag held the doctor back for a minute or two. Standing there in the darkness of the trees, they observed a remarkable drama.

Five or six men were busy demolishing the old pavilion by the light of a few torches that had been placed in a circle around them in the snow. The roof had already been removed along with some of the walls. Calling out to one another playfully, the fellows were breaking up the dark timber and stacking the planks in a pile.

A fur-clad, white-bearded gentleman strode back and forth excitably, observing the activity. He issued a stream of orders and urged on the men as one might urge on a pack of hunting dogs. The men laughed as they worked, as if they thought this was the most tremendous fun. Asbjørn Krag was reminded of the driver's smile: They all take the old man for a lunatic, he thought.

Now the doctor pointed at the white-bearded man in furs and whispered:

"There he is—that is Aakerholm."

"I thought as much," Krag replied.

Just then, the old man forced his way in among the men and shouted: "Tear up the floor! Hurry now, the floor…"

At that very moment, Krag spied a figure he had not seen before. The detective hastily hid behind a tree so that he could stand there and covertly observe the others. He realized at once that the newcomer must be the adopted son, Bengt. He was wearing hunting dress, and high, fur-lined boots. He stood there quite calmly, watching the hustle and bustle with the indifference of a person observing other people's labour. He was puffing on a cigar and his face bore an expression that was utterly devoid of interest. All this Asbjørn Krag noted as he stood behind the tree trunk. But suddenly, something happened that sent a shiver down the detective's spine.

Bengt had caught sight of the doctor, who was so absorbed by the sight of old Aakerholm that he had eyes for nothing else. Asbjørn Krag saw how the young man's face abruptly altered, how he directed a scrutinizing, hateful gaze at the doctor. The first sign, thought Krag, and stepped out of his hiding place. As he did so, Bengt went over to the doctor, throwing away his cigar and reaching out a hand in greeting.

"Welcome back, Doctor," he said. "I hear you have been in the capital, sir. I take it this gentleman is the specialist?"

"Dr Krag, Bengt Aakerholm," the doctor said in introduction, then asked: "What in the world is going on here?"

"Somebody tried to shoot father," Bengt answered.

"Tried to shoot him?"

"Yes—or so he says at least."

Just then the old man himself came up to them.

"It was only by the grace of God that he missed me," he shouted, bewildered and nervous. "I got a pretty good look at him—he came out of the door of the pavilion and when I started to run after him, he fired a pistol at me."

"Why did you run after him?"

The old man threw a swift glance at the detective and replied, "Because I saw that he had it in for me, of course. This isn't my first brush with a murderer, my dear sir."

Krag nodded.

"I see, but he didn't hit you."

"No, but after firing at me, he dashed back into the pavilion."

"And you?"

"I ran up to the manor for help. The first person I met was my son Bengt. He hurried down to the pavilion at once."

"Ah, he did, did he?" the detective said. "But by then the bird had flown?"

"No," the old man replied sharply. "Because there were no tracks in the snow leading away from the pavilion."

"But nor was there any murderer to be found in the pavilion, Father," Bengt objected. "I believe you are mistaken, sir."

"I am not mistaken," the old man said. He turned on his heel and walked, silent and brooding, towards the manor. The doctor accompanied him, leaving Asbjørn Krag and Bengt to walk together.

"What is your opinion on this matter?" asked the detective.

Bengt replied evasively: "Poor Father."

34

"You think it is a figment of his imagination."

"I do. Does that not seem reasonable to you too?"

"Most definitely not. I believe that strange things are afoot here."

"You are quick to reach your conclusion, sir."

"I have already familiarised myself with the entire case."

"But surely we can assume that I know my stepfather better than you, who have barely set eyes on him. And I am convinced that the whole thing is in his mind. I have been convinced of it from the very first moment."

"Really? Even this evening when the old man came back to the manor and said someone had tried to shoot him?"

"Yes."

"Was the old man very agitated when he told you?"

"Extremely agitated."

"That being so, it seems most odd to me that you dashed off to the pavilion instead of staying to calm the old man down. Considering that you thought it was all in his mind, I mean."

Bengt looked surprised again. "I always know what I'm doing," he replied.

"I believe you do. And you were the first person to reach the pavilion, I suppose?"

"Yes, but I didn't find a single living soul in there."

"And I presume you noticed at once that there were no tracks in the snow leading away from the pavilion."

"I saw it instantly."

"And were you the one who told the old man this?"

35

"Yes."

At that, Asbjørn Krag stopped and laid a hand half-playfully upon the other man's shoulder. In an urgent, confidential tone, he said: "Come now, my dear fellow, admit it. There *were* tracks leading away from the pavilion."

Bengt started in astonishment and took a step back, hissing an oath.

"What tracks are you talking about?"

But Krag answered quite calmly, "Why your own, my dear fellow. Your own tracks."

"What the devil—mine?"

Krag did not reply at once, but gave Bengt a long look. It was clear enough that the young man was suppressing an intense indignation. Krag suddenly burst out laughing— hearty uproarious laughter.

"But of course," he said. "Your tracks must have led away from the pavilion. You had been inside, after all, hadn't you? How else could you assure me that there wasn't a living soul in the pavilion?"

Now Bengt laughed too, although in a forced manner. And both gentlemen were still laughing as they entered the manor, as if they had shared some pleasant joke.

When all four gentlemen were gathered in old Aakerholm's parlour some minutes later, Asbjørn Krag was able to confirm what he had surmised all along: that Bengt was a thoroughly charmless young fellow. A well-fed giant of a man, some thirty years of age with a full head of hair, he sprinkled his speech liberally with foreign words in a pretentious, uncultured fashion. As for the old man, the detective warmed to him enormously at once and felt very sorry for him indeed. The old man looked so exhausted and dishevelled, but was silent and withdrawn.

"My dear Father," Bengt said. "You should do as I shall—go to bed at once. Take my advice, as your sole and truest friend."

But Bengt's apparent calm was belied by his behaviour when he left the room a moment later: He slammed the door so hard behind him that it made the walls shake. Shortly afterwards, the old man also said goodnight. When he had gone, the doctor remarked: "Now he will go through his three rooms where no one may follow him. What do you think?"

The detective answered, "I believe he is doomed. What a strange place I have come to, among strange people."

A servant showed the gentlemen to the guest rooms on the second floor. The doctor threw himself wearily on his bed at once. But Asbjørn Krag was now livelier and more alert than ever.

"I suppose you are well acquainted with the manor?" he asked. "Can we see the old man's room from here?"

The doctor got up and walked over to the window.

"Look," he answered, pointing. "See those windows at the end of the second floor in that wing over there? Those are the three rooms."

A light shone in the last of the windows. Suddenly it went out.

"Now the old man is settling for the night," Krag remarked. Turning to the doctor, he continued: "There is something you must do before you go to bed."

"With pleasure, if it is within my power."

"You must go down and fetch the dog."

Krag pointed down into the courtyard, where a coal-black shadow padded back and forth in the darkness.

"Why?"

"It is necessary."

The doctor left.

A few minutes later, Krag heard muffled growls from the courtyard. Then all was silent. Shortly afterwards the doctor returned with the dog, which was wagging its tail affectionately. It knew the doctor.

Krag waited another half-an-hour. By then, all the lights in the manor's many windows were out.

The detective placed a revolver in his pocket and stole out into the darkness. After making his way down a complex series of staircases, he lifted a door off its hinges as swiftly and expertly as a burglar, and soon found himself outside in the open air. He drank the chill air down in great draughts, for it really had grown very cold; silent and cold. The air nipped sharply at his ears and the cold seized hold of the old building, pressing it so hard that its joints creaked here and there.

Blessing the darkness, Asbjørn Krag stole carefully along the wall of the manor until he found himself directly below the three rooms. The detective noticed that the ground floor of the wing was a storeroom piled high with boxes and bales. Next came the old man's rooms. Above that, an uninhabited loft. The most thorough isolation, thought Krag. He waited there for a few minutes, listening. But no noise reached him down there. An iron drainpipe ran down one corner of the wing, from roof to ground. Krag tried to climb it, but failed at first, sliding back down. On his second attempt, however, and with superhuman effort, he managed to climb as high as the upper part of the ground floor window frame.

Suddenly, he heard a distant cry or shout. The cry seemed to come from a long way off, as if from some abyss. He clung fast to the iron drainpipe and listened. And now, the cry came again. All at once an idea raced through Krag's mind, making his heart miss a beat: The shout had come from Aakerholm's room; that is what a cry sounds like through padded walls, he thought. He listened again and then he heard someone shouting, but infinitely far off, infinitely remote: "Take that, you devil…"

At once Krag slid back down, so fast that his fingers left shreds of skin on the drainpipe. He walked back the way he had come, but at a quicker pace. He reached the door, which he had lifted off its hinges, and put it back in place as quietly as he could.

But just as he was about to close the door and go up to his room, he heard someone on the stairs. A person who must have seen his silhouette in the doorway against the white snow.

CHAPTER 3

THE SHOTS

Asbjørn Krag stepped backwards to lean against the wall; then he stood completely still. A coal-black darkness enveloped him. He could see nothing but the bluish sheen of the snow in the doorway. Yet he sensed that someone was nearby. Two minutes passed and nothing happened.

Then, all of a sudden, the detective heard dry, scornful laughter right by his ear. He gave a start.

"What is the doctor doing out so late at night?" The mocking tones of Bengt reached him from the darkness.

But now that Asbjørn Krag knew who the stranger was, he quickly recovered his steely presence of mind.

"Surely you can see for yourself, sir," he replied.

Now Bengt walked past the detective, approaching the open door. Krag noticed that he was still in hunting dress. So he had not gone to bed, thought the detective. A bag with a leather strap hung from his shoulder. He had a rifle beneath his arm.

"Out hunting so late?" Krag asked.

But Bengt did not reply. He stood there in the doorway, looking scornfully at Krag.

"I am the one asking questions here," he said. "What are you doing out so late, Doctor? Surely you weren't lured out by the pavilion?"

Asbjørn Krag seized upon the idea at once.

"Indeed I was," he answered. "I went out to look at the pavilion—because I really do believe some living soul tried to shoot your stepfather. And then, just as I was about to settle for the night, it occurred to me: What if there *were* some hiding place in the foundations of the pavilion? After all, the labourers forgot to demolish them."

"But was it really necessary to break down the door in order to get there?"

"I had no key. Besides, a locked door is a mere trifle for me."

"You behave like a burglar, Doctor."

"Or a detective," Krag replied with a loud laugh.

Pursing his lips tightly, Bengt started to fiddle with his rifle, weighing it pointedly on his arm.

"When one sees a man break in through doors like that on a dark night," he said, "it is hard to assume he is anything other than a criminal. I might easily have shot you, Doctor."

"This isn't the first time I have looked down the barrel of a gun."

"I'm sure. I say this only to encourage you to be more cautious."

At that, Asbjørn Krag laughed once more.

"Next time, you mean, sir—next time, I shan't be spared

a bullet."

"In my view, you would do well pay attention to good advice. Would you be so kind as to let the dog loose again? Goodnight."

Bengt slung the rifle over his shoulder and headed towards the woods, the trampled snow creaking beneath his feet.

Asbjørn Krag returned to his room, where the doctor awaited him apprehensively.

"I heard voices. Who were you talking to?"

"Bengt," Krag replied.

"Did he go out?"

Krag nodded.

"Where to?"

The detective pointed towards the forest, which surged towards the manor like a vast, dark ocean.

"Did you find anything?"

"Yes."

"Anything important?"

"Yes."

"Was I right to bring you here?"

"I am very grateful that you did."

"The old fellow is not just hallucinating then?"

"Most definitely not."

Krag was perfectly calm; no one could have told from looking at him that he had just experienced a moment of violent tension. He stood with his hands behind his back warming himself at the hearth.

"A vile crime is being planned," he said. "And heaven knows, it may even have been executed."

At these words, the doctor leapt to his feet and stared into the detective's eyes with a terrified gaze.

"Who is the criminal?"

"I have no idea yet, but I shall find out by tomorrow. For now, old sawbones, all we can do is take things easy. Let the dog out, Doctor, and tend to these hands of mine."

Smiling, the detective held out both hands. The fingers were bloody.

* * *

When the doctor awoke at nine the next morning, Asbjørn Krag was just returning from a brisk walk. The detective joked and laughed and was in excellent humour.

"What delightful winter weather!" he cried out. "And what a marvellous landscape."

The doctor at once leapt out from beneath his eiderdown.

"You're in a good mood today." he said. "Is everything in order?"

"Everything is in order. The old man is in splendid spirits and already much recovered from yesterday's events. But heavens, how these terrors affect him. Incidentally, if you wish to know why I am in such good humour, it is because I have uncovered the secret of the three rooms."

"Impossible! When did you find that out?"

"Last night, after you had fallen asleep."

"Did something else happen last night?"

"No, but I sat up in that big chair mulling over the case; I smoked and thought and smoked. And suddenly, it became clear to me all at once."

"You are tormenting me. Krag, what is the nature of the secret?"

"I cannot explain it to you yet. You must be tormented a little while longer. You will simply have to put up with it."

"And the crime?"

"It is being planned. But it no longer has any connection to the three rooms. We have emerged from one mystery only to find ourselves embroiled in another. Let us go down and have breakfast now."

The detective and the doctor ate with old Aakerholm and his adopted son. Asbjørn Krag was on excellent form and the old man was greatly tickled by his many odd witticisms. Even Bengt seemed keen to be reconciled with him.

The day passed without any remarkable events. Just after midday, a man arrived with a box for Asbjørn Krag. The detective said it contained books.

"I become so greatly absorbed in my studies," he said, "that I must have my books with me even on my travels." He had the box taken up to his room at once.

The doctor observed this little drama with surprise. He knew that Asbjørn Krag rarely troubled himself with any reading beyond legal documents. The doctor guessed that there was some secret here and as soon as the detective vanished to his room, the doctor followed.

When he came into Krag's room, the detective had already opened the box.

"Shut the door behind you!" he shouted to the doctor.

"What on earth are you up to?" the doctor asked, with curious interest.

"I am putting my books in order," Krag answered.

The doctor moved closer. The box contained nothing but glass. But Krag picked up the pieces of glass one after another, handling them as gently and carefully as one might handle the finest volumes in a bookshop.

"Don't you see what it is?" Krag asked, as, with an eager whistle, he picked a new piece of glass out of the box and examined it very closely. "These are all the shards of the mirror that the old man shattered."

"How on earth did you get your hands on them?"

"One of the first things I investigated this morning was, of course, whether all the fragments of the mirror still existed. And they did. The stable boy had taken care of them. So I got a travelling rag-and-bone man to buy the pieces and then send them to me in this box. I am a master of such small arrangements, my dear Doctor. I could not, of course, have asked to have the fragments delivered to me as it would have attracted too much attention."

The detective counted.

"Yes, here they all are, it seems. I shall soon have the mirror back in one piece."

He stood gazing at the pieces of glass and shook his head.

"A peculiar mirror," he murmured. "A most peculiar mirror."

* * *

When the coffee had been drunk, the lamps lit, and the cigars placed upon the table, the old man gradually began to unbend. Asbjørn Krag left him and the doctor sitting deep in conversation, while he exchanged a few private words with Bengt.

Asbjørn Krag asked what the lady who was betrothed to old Aakerholm was like.

Bengt offered a description that coincided in the most important respects with the one the doctor had provided.

"So she is still relatively young and beautiful?"

"Yes."

Krag gave Bengt a penetrating look, but asked his questions in a half-joking tone.

"Wouldn't she make a better match for you?"

Bengt tried to rise to break off the conversation but Krag held him back.

"In my view, you see," he continued, "your stepfather is quite honestly too old to remarry."

"I share that view," Bengt answered.

"In that case, you should work diligently against his marriage plans. And you have probably done so, have you not?"

Bengt hesitated before answering. At last he said: "Of course I have opposed the old man. But," he added in his oddly pretentious manner, "mine has been a gentlemanly, polite opposition."

Bengt really did use the word "gentleman" rather too often and in all kinds of situations.

Krag continued, unmoved: "From a strictly financial standpoint, you would also benefit if this marriage failed to take place. The inheritance... "

But now Bengt got up in earnest and stalked off wearing an expression that suggested he wished to say: "Heavens, what an oaf."

Just then, the doctor laughed loudly at one of Aakerholm's tales. By now he was out on the prairie, tumbling around with wild horses, buffalo herds and Native Americans.

"No word of a lie," he embellished eagerly. "I aimed at his left eye and hit him smack in the pupil from two hundred feet."

Asbjørn Krag approached the group and asked quietly: "Excuse me—was that with a revolver?"

On hearing this, the old man hurled himself back in his chair, guffawing.

"Well, will you just listen to that!" he cried. "Listen to that greenhorn—it was a rifle of course, you gosh-darned fool!"

Aakerholm had a particularly blunt way of expressing himself when excitable, but it seemed to make no impact on Asbjørn Krag, who simply replied with barely concealed contempt, "Aha, I see."

The old man became angrier and angrier.

"Just listen to that chicken," he mocked. "Hear it cluck! Have you even smelt gunpowder before, sir?"

"Revolver shooting is my sole hobby," Krag answered. "And I am an excellent shot with a revolver."

"Now that I have to see."

"I am happy to oblige whenever you please. Could you gentlemen wait a moment?" he asked, then left the room.

He returned at once holding the little black box. He opened it and took out two revolvers, a pair of astonishingly small gold-plated guns.

The old man simmered down at the sight of the weapons, which he studied with attention and interest, holding them gently in his hand. He seemed afraid that they might fall to pieces—the work was that fine.

"Let's see you shoot!" he shouted, handing one of the revolvers to the detective and keeping the other himself.

Krag fastened a piece of paper to the thick, solid oak plank that served as the doorstep leading onto the veranda.

Then he went far into the adjoining room directly opposite, briefly took aim and fired.

The bullet hit the piece of paper. It was a good shot. The old man got up eagerly and seemed almost ready to embrace Krag.

"I do beg your pardon!" he shouted. "Forgive me! That was an excellent shot. Let me try now."

Aakerholm's face had regained its former healthy colour and the old man's eyes shone. He inhaled the smell of gunpowder like an animal scenting food.

He placed himself in the same spot where Krag had stood and fired.

His bullet also hit the paper.

"I take my hat off," Krag said with a bow. The old man bowed again and for a while they entertained themselves exchanging playful compliments.

"A card!" the old man shouted suddenly. "Give me a card." He was given a playing card, which he fastened to the oak plank. It was a three of spades. Then he fired and hit the edge of the card.

After that, Asbjørn Krag fired three shots in quick succession. The doctor removed the card and it turned out that Krag had picked off all three spades on the card.

Bengt looked at the detective in astonishment and dismay. But the old man threw the beautiful little revolver on the floor scornfully.

"Modern trash!" he bellowed. "Away with it! Wait here, gentlemen, and you shall see me shoot with my own pistol, my very own old pistol."

There was a strange melancholy ring to the old man's voice, as if he were speaking of a beloved child now dead.

The doctor observed Asbjørn Krag attentively. All at once he realized that the detective had planned this whole drama. What was he up to? Asbjørn Krag's face betrayed a tremendous tension, and the doctor had the distinct impression that something was about to happen.

CHAPTER 4

THE SECRET IN THE BOOK

E veryone waited in suspense for the old man's return.
Bengt stood staring at the playing card, whose three
spades Asbjørn Krag had picked off with his bullets. He
marvelled at these shooting skills. Unnoticed by the others, Krag had pushed his chair closer to the place where
Aakerholm had been sitting.

At last, the old man returned, eager and uttering
mild oaths.

When he appeared in the doorway, he exclaimed: "Take
a look at this, sir: now that's what I call a weapon!"

And he showed them a big double-barrelled pistol of
old-fashioned construction.

He jokingly took aim at them one after another.
Asbjørn Krag, who was sitting closest to him, had the pistol's two barrels thrust right in his face.

"It's loaded," the old man shouted with a laugh. "Mind
yourselves, mind yourselves. If you don't sit quietly, I'll
shave off your eyelashes with a shot. This here gun is in
a different league from that dainty little revolver of yours,
Doctor."

Aakerholm gave a scornful kick to one of Krag's revolvers, which had fallen on the floor. Then he went over and fixed a new playing card to the doorstep, an ace of hearts. He fired at it from inside the adjacent room and hit the ace.

Now both rooms were filled with gunpowder smoke. But the old man seemed to thrive on the sharp stench. Proudly, he walked up to Asbjørn Krag to receive acknowledgement of his splendid sharp shooting.

But Krag just sat there in his chair, quite calm and unmoved. He asked to take a look at the pistol, which the old man handed to him.

The detective weighed it pensively in his hand and read an inscription on the silver grip without any particular interest; but then, all of a sudden, he looked at Aakerholm gravely and said, "Ah, so this is the pistol."

Seemingly thunderstruck, the old man stared at the detective with terrified, wide-open eyes and stammered: "What... what do you mean, sir?"

But now Krag was completely indifferent once more.

"What do I mean?" he replied. "Why, nothing in particular. All I meant to say was: So this is your pistol. You're a fine shot, sir."

Old Aakerholm did not answer, but gazed at Krag for almost half a minute, with an attentive, searching expression. When at last he sat down in his big armchair, there was a strange look of surprise on his haggard old face.

Two servants now opened up windows and doors, and the gunpowder smoke swept out in great wafts. Almost all the maids and menservants had come running in the greatest alarm when they heard the shots. Asbjørn Krag could tell from their faces that all were convinced some accident had occurred. Bengt waved them all away, but the corridors were full of chatter about the five shots and their lunatic of a master. Everyone now seemed to agree that the old man must be mad.

"The doctor and Bengt were terrified," said Andresen, a Swissman, who had been the first of the serving staff to arrive. "But did you all see that new gentleman, the stranger? He must be an odd fish because he sat there quite calmly, puffing away at his cigar as the bullets flew all around him."

"And then he laughed at us when we came running," another servant added.

"Who do you think did the shooting?"

"It must have been the old boy."

"Maybe it was Bengt."

The buzz of questions and answers continued long into the night in the kitchen and the servants' quarters. Everyone agreed that things were getting downright sinister here at the old manor.

In the meantime, the four gentlemen had resumed their conversations. The room still smelt of burnt gunpowder, so Asbjørn Krag suggested they go into the other room.

But this idea instantly provoked strong opposition from Bengt. Krag noticed it and thought it strange.

"Why should we move? Isn't it pleasant enough in here?"

Bengt said in a somewhat irascible tone. "Besides, Father likes the smell of gunpowder. He doesn't suffer the excessive refinement of us city types."

Krag smiled faintly at Bengt's last remark. But the old man agreed with his adopted son.

"Let's stay where we are," he said. "I think it's nice here."

And so they stayed.

Krag sat almost buried in his armchair. He puffed and puffed away, cocooning himself in a dense fog of cigar smoke, which rose up to the ceiling like a cloud. Dr Rasch observed him with unswerving attention. The detective's eyes were half shut as if, defeated by tiredness, he were drifting off to sleep. But the doctor realized that this was precisely when Krag was paying sharpest heed to everything he saw and heard around him.

Bengt began to wander to and fro, making small talk. He spoke to the old man and the doctor about ships and shipping, complaining bitterly about the poor coal freight from England. Asbjørn Krag interjected a word here and there, demonstrating that he too was familiar that branch of industry; the doctor was almost becoming bored.

On one occasion, as he walked back and forth across the room, Bengt stopped in front of Asbjørn Krag.

"Are you tired?" he asked. "Wouldn't it be best if you turned in?"

"No thank you," Krag responded flatly. "It is just a moment's weariness."

"That," said Bengt sarcastically, "is what comes of not

using the night for sleeping."

"Perhaps."

During all this idle chatter, the doctor felt an unbearable tension. He realized that Asbjørn Krag's tiredness was feigned. But why? What did he have in mind? And what was the meaning of that scene with the pistol? Why had old Aakerholm been so puzzled and alarmed by the detective's perfectly innocent remark? And why didn't Bengt wish to leave this room with its stench of gunpowder? The doctor thought and pondered, but the more he thought, the more mysterious it all seemed to him. However, he had no opportunity to brood further on the matter, because now the following occurred.

Asbjørn Krag, who had been totally silent for almost ten minutes, suddenly asked: "Listen here, Aakerholm. Are you quite certain you saw a man over by the pavilion aiming a gun at you yesterday evening?"

The doctor saw that the question took the old man by surprise and it embarrassed him to answer.

"Absolutely certain," Aakerholm replied.

Krag continued to puff on his twelfth cigar for a few seconds, then asked again: "What was he wearing?"

The old man started visibly. He was quiet for a long time, but in the end he answered, in some confusion: "I don't recall. I can't say. Besides, I find it unpleasant to talk about these matters, and it's hardly necessary, is it?" He stood up and went over to his writing desk, where he busied himself leafing through some papers.

"Quite so," Krag answered, indifferent as before. "Ah, well, I have learned enough now anyway."

Suddenly the old man gave a cry, a cry of terror. He buried his face abruptly in his hands, but then raised his head again just as swiftly, trying to hide his movement. The doctor's first instinct was to hurry over to him but a glance from Asbjørn Krag stopped him in his tracks. Bengt had gone into the adjoining room just moments before.

The old man crumpled a piece of paper in his hand and started to leaf through a book feverishly. The doctor could not see his face but from the way the old man's back shuddered, he could tell that Aakerholm was in a state of the utmost agitation.

From his vantage point, however, Asbjørn Krag could see across the writing desk, and through his half-open lids, his eyes followed every one of the old man's movements. Aakerholm leafed back and forth in the book, quickly and feverishly. At last, he seemed to have found what he was seeking, for he muttered a single sentence to himself. Then he quickly snapped the book shut, threw it down on the desk, got up and left the room, pale and tremulous. The doctor followed him, but not before observing that Asbjørn Krag had plucked up the book with the practised ease of a pickpocket. The doctor took Aakerholm by the arm. On the threshold, he met Bengt, now dressed in a fur coat and cap. The whole peculiar scene had lasted barely two minutes.

When the doctor returned a moment later, he found

Asbjørn Krag and Bengt talking quietly together.

With a smile, Krag asked the doctor: "Well, then—did you follow him through the three rooms?"

"No," the doctor replied. "He slammed the door unceremoniously in my face."

The detective laughed out loud and turned to Bengt.

"You father became tired," he said. "I see you are in furs. Are you on your way out?"

"I'm going to the club," Bengt answered.

Krag stretched his arms and yawned with boredom.

"My, how I wish I could join you."

"Be my guest—there is nothing to stop you. Listen! The sleigh-bells are already jingling at the door. Dr Rasch?"

"No," the detective answered swiftly. "The doctor would rather remain here tonight."

"Yes, I'd prefer to stay here," the doctor added, with a touch of perplexity.

When, some minutes later, the detective went out to the sleigh with Bengt, the doctor realized that Asbjørn Krag had seen through the whole game, and a happy calm settled over his mind.

* * *

A motley group of people was gathered at the little town's club. Krag and Bengt had arrived so late that signs of drunkenness were already evident here and there. Bengt's arrival was greeted with rejoicing, which the vain young man received with a smile.

Krag rapidly found himself seated among a number of the town's dignitaries. There was a portly, constantly tippling mayor with blue folds behind his ears, whose fat and bloated face was flushed and shiny—a clear case of galloping apoplexy. Then there was the police inspector, popularly known as "Polly", an idle prattler, with the pallid plumpness of a toper. He sat safely ensconced in his chair, alternately sipping from his glass and answering any question that came his way with "indubitably," "indubitably". Next was a young social climber of a lawyer, who was given to extravagant gestures and lengthy speeches. Beside him sat a former mayor. Krag realized that he had stumbled upon a political gathering, for he heard the former mayor whisper, "We shall probably undermine—". It appeared to be an opposition club, some kind of progressive association.

Now and then Bengt joined the party, raised his glass in a toast, was praised and left again.

"An excellent man," said the former mayor. "He's a clever chap, a skilled man."

"Indubitably," interjected Polly.

The Apoplectic also bellowed his approval.

But immediately afterwards, the lawyer said: "It seems he is at odds with his stepfather, however. He isn't keen on the old man's plans to marry the Silken Girl. But the less said about that the better."

"Indubitably," said Polly, sipping from his glass.

All at once, the little clique put their heads together over the table. Krag heard them speaking about "the Silken

Girl" and he caught a remark from the lawyer, "Mightn't Bengt himself…?"

When, just then, Bengt approached the table with a smile on his face, the lawyer got up and addressed a speech to him: The town's bright young hope, the pillar of the party. Bengt thanked him and said, "We gentlemen…," but Krag heard no more because he left the group in boredom and went over to another table.

But drunkenness and politicking were everywhere in evidence, for the elections were imminent and it was important to stick together.

Some youths were amusing themselves in an adjoining room—a much younger group of grocers, lieutenants and newly minted consuls. Someone was playing the piano.

All of a sudden, a burst of laughter came from this room and a few young men came storming out to tell everyone what had happened.

Old Captain Evensen, drunk as usual, had managed to mislay a pint of beer in the piano: He had been standing there, waving his arms in time with the pianist, when he inadvertently dropped the bottle of beer he was drinking into the open piano. The bottle had snapped two strings and was now lodged so deep inside the piano that it was impossible to retrieve. This event provoked several minutes of riotous amusement.

But then the lawyer took the floor and delivered a patriotic speech. The elections were close at hand and the most vital interests of the fatherland were at stake. So moving was the speech that all those present agreed to sing the national anthem. The pianist launched into the tune, but produced the most peculiar notes because Evensen's beer had seeped between the keys, making them so tacky that they stuck together. Meanwhile Polly, the lawyer, the former mayor, the Apoplectic and the rest linked their arms to form a fraternal, staggering chain.

Just then, the door was flung open and a youngish grocer hurried in, calling for silence. He was pale, agitated and sober. All eyes fell upon him. Krag realized that the man had a serious message to convey and was overcome by a terrible foreboding that made him shudder.

"Gentlemen," shouted the newcomer. "Our town and district have suffered a dreadful loss. I have just received a telephone call from Kvamberg. Old Aakerholm died some minutes ago. His body was found in the grounds of the estate."

The silence that followed this awful news was broken by the smash of a glass on the floor—Bengt's glass. Krag looked at the man, as he slumped pallid against the doorpost.

CHAPTER 5

THE DEAD MAN

When Asbjørn Krag and Bengt returned to Kvamberg after a breakneck sleigh ride, they found the manor ablaze with lights, lit up as if for a party. The two men had exchanged few words during their headlong journey. But Bengt did make one remark that caught the detective's attention.

"Was the body found in the grounds? That is peculiar."

The sleigh glided up to the main entrance and the doctor came out of the mansion, ashen and bareheaded. He was so agitated that he could barely speak. Neither did Krag ask him any questions.

Some of the servants came outside to help Bengt and Krag out of the sleigh. Close by some women stood with their heads in their hands, sobbing. The fat, sturdy Swissman went over to hush them.

"Where is the body?" asked Bengt as he made his way through the servants.

"In the parlour," someone replied.

Bengt went first, with Asbjørn Krag and the doctor close behind. Along the way, they met more weeping women. The doctor caught a remark from one of them: "Ah, the master has done himself a mischief."

Krag sent a surprised and enquiring glance to the doctor, who sighed.

"Shot himself," he whispered. "Shot himself in the heart."

The detective hastened his steps and entered the parlour ahead of Bengt. There on the table lay the corpse, covered in a white sheet.

Bengt made to run over and tear off the sheet, but Krag restrained him.

"Can you bear to see a corpse?" he asked.

Bengt measured him disdainfully with his eyes and answered: "Do you think this is the time for jokes?"

"Joke or not, it is the doctor's business to deal with the body. The deceased shot himself, after all."

"Shot himself!" Bengt cried. "That is impossible. I thought it was a stroke."

"So did I," said Asbjørn Krag quietly, as he uncovered the body. Now the doctor stepped up too. The detective arranged the sheet so that the dead man's face remained hidden.

Old Aakerholm was dressed in his ordinary clothes and coat. He lay on his back, his right hand clutching the pistol he had fired with such astonishing accuracy earlier that evening. Traces of the fatal bullet were clearly visible on the dead man's clothing.

"Straight to the heart," the doctor whispered. "The old chap certainly knew where to aim."

Bengt had stood silent for several minutes. Now, as he bowed over the dead man, he suddenly burst out "Oh my poor white-haired father! So this is how you decided to seek peace."

Audible sobs came from the doorway, which was filled with the servants' faces.

Just then, Asbjørn Krag removed the sheet from the dead man's face. Bengt leapt backwards, hands outstretched before him as if to ward off a horrible sight.

No wonder—for old Aakerholm's face was enough to make the strongest man tremble.

It had stiffened into an expression of the ghastliest terror: his eyes protruded from their sockets, his mouth was twisted. What had the unfortunate soul seen the instant before his death?

"Cover him up again," Bengt urged. "His face is so dreadful."

Asbjørn Krag dropped the sheet back over the distorted features at once. Then he pried the pistol from the grasp of the cold fingers and examined it more closely. It was indeed the same double-barrelled pistol that Aakerholm had used earlier that evening.

"No one must touch the body," he ordered sternly. "It must remain in precisely this position until I say otherwise."

At first, Bengt seemed put out by Krag's authoritative tone, but he pulled himself together at once and told his servants: "Do as he says."

Turning to Krag, he continued, "I authorize you to do

whatever you deem necessary in this matter."

Krag nodded indifferently.

"Please ensure that a fast horse and sleigh are at the ready," he said. "I must send a few telegrams."

He pointed towards the door.

"Show these inquisitive souls out—they have no business here. And show in the person or persons who found the body."

"I was the first to reach the body," the Swissman said, stepping into the room with a grave and heavy tread.

"And I heard both shots," said another fellow, a stable boy, as he followed the Swissman in.

"Both?" Bengt and Krag exclaimed together, equally surprised. "Were there two shots?"

"Yes," answered the doctor, who was now almost himself again. "Two shots were heard."

"Good," said Krag. "Shut the door."

The maids and menservants left and the door was shut.

Asbjørn dealt with the stable boy first.

"So you were the one who heard the two shots?" he asked.

"That I was."

"Where were you at the time?"

"I'd just mucked out the horses and locked the stable door."

"What time was it?"

"The clock in the tower had just struck eleven. I remember because I stood there and counted every stroke."

"Were you alone?"

"Yes, I was on my own."

"Are you certain that no one else was in the vicinity?"

"I'm sure of it. The moon was shining brightly out there and I'd have seen if anyone was nearby."

"And then you heard the shots?"

"Yes. That's when I heard the first shot."

"Could you tell right away where it came from?"

"Yes. I knew at once that the shot was fired out in the grounds."

"What did you do next?"

"I was pretty scared at first but then I ran across the yard and yelled for Andresen, the Swissman. It was after I'd called for him that I heard the second shot."

"How much time elapsed between the two shots?"

"Only a few seconds. Not even half a minute, I'd say."

"Was there any difference between the sound of the shots? I mean, was one of them louder than the other?"

The stable boy thought it over.

"I can't say for sure," he said. "But it seems to me, now you're asking, that the first shot was louder than the second. The second one sounded like it came from further off."

Now the doctor joined the conversation.

"But it doesn't make any sense—how could there be two shots?" he said. "There was only one bullet in the body."

Bengt, who had stood by the window gazing out at the moonlight during the whole of Krag's conversation with the stable boy, turned around abruptly on hearing the stable boy's observation.

"It is a fact, Doctor," he said "as you should know, that suicides often fire a trial shot in the air. It's a way of summoning up the courage to go through with the deed."

"Indeed, there have been many such instances," Krag murmured.

"And besides," Bengt continued, "might it not be possible that the poor man first tried to shoot himself in the head but missed."

"Do you think he tended to miss?" Krag asked.

"Anyone's hands might tremble at such a moment," Bengt said, picking the pistol up off the table. "At any rate, he fired from both barrels, because they are empty."

"I saw that already," Krag answered. "Which makes the mystery even darker."

Then the detective turned to the stable boy.

"What did you do next?"

"The Swissman, Andresen, came running down to me after I'd called him. I told him about the shots and then we both went out into the grounds. But first Andresen told the other servants."

"Did you find the body at once?" the detective asked Andresen.

"No," Andresen replied. "Not right away. We searched for more than ten minutes, shouting as we went. In the end, I saw something dark by one of the trees a few paces away from the road and went over there. It was the master. I shook him but he was dead. He's probably killed himself,

I thought at once, because I saw the pistol in his hand straight away. I called the stable boy and a couple of other manservants who had arrived in the meantime and then we carried the body up here. That's all I know."

Asbjørn Krag stood thinking for a while. Then he asked:

"Did any of you see Aakerholm after we drove into town?"

"I went to my room immediately," said the doctor. "So I didn't see him. I thought the old fellow had gone to bed."

"Mariane saw him," Andresen answered.

"Who is Mariane?"

"The parlour maid."

"Call her in!"

A moment later, Mariane arrived—a red-haired woman aged over thirty. Her eyes were still wet with tears.

"I hear that you were the last person to see Aakerholm," Krag began.

"I saw him walking about," Mariane answered. "I'd gone into the parlour to tidy up. He came in while I was doing that."

"Did he say anything?"

"He asked me if the gentlemen had really gone to the club. I answered that I didn't know where they'd gone but they'd just driven off with Blakken."

"I see—go on."

"Then he started looking for something."

"Looking for something?"

"Yes, for a book."

Asbjørn Krag and the doctor exchanged a swift glance.

"Did he find it?" asked Krag.

"No and he was very cross about it. He cursed something rotten. 'It was here just a moment ago,' he said. 'Is everything in this house bewitched?' He spent more than a quarter of an hour looking but he didn't find the book. But…"

Bengt suddenly interrupted again.

"What did you say?" he cried. "He didn't find the book?" But then he pulled himself together abruptly and added. "Ah, no—never mind. I was thinking of something else."

Asbjørn Krag looked sharply at Bengt, who avoided his gaze.

Mariane continued.

"But he did find… er…"

She started to tremble and was once again on the point of tears.

"What did he find?"

Mariane pointed at the pistol and stammered in fear and horror: "That… that thing there."

"Ah, the pistol."

"Yes. 'Is that still here?' he said, and put it in his coat pocket. Then he went out."

"Down into the grounds?"

Mariane became uncertain.

"No… he went in the opposite direction, along the little avenue of trees."

"Don't you find it odd that he went out so late?"

"No, I don't."

"Why not?"

It took almost a minute for Mariane to answer. Then, as if embarrassed, she said: "Because he went along the little avenue."

Bengt again interjected.

"I see no point in such a painstaking interrogation." he said. "It is harrowing for both me and the staff."

Asbjørn paid no attention to him but continued to question Mariane.

"Where does that avenue lead to?"

"It leads to… to the Hjelm house."

"Ah, now I understand—to the Silken Girl. To Aakerholm's betrothed."

"Yes," replied Mariane. "Widow Hjelm lives close by with her mother."

"That is excellent. Thank you. I have no further need of you."

Mariane, Andresen and the stable boy all left. But as they reached the door, they all cast timid glances at the table where Aakerholm's corpse lay beneath the white sheet.

When the servants had gone, Krag went over to the dead man.

"With your permission," he said to Bengt, "I wish to take the old man's keys."

"What do you plan to do with them?"

"We need them."

"Why?"

"Because we shall now walk through the three rooms, of course."

"But is that respectful to the dead man?" Bengt objected.

"It must be done."

"Well, then," replied the young man. "Let us do it."

Krag took the keys.

The doctor inwardly admired Krag's phenomenal calm and certainty. Now he was in his element, now he was at work. He spoke and acted without hesitation. Although he was slightly pale, nothing in his stony face betrayed any sign of unease or agitation. But his eyes glowed and glinted like a cat's in the darkness.

"Look," whispered Bengt, as he pointed out of the window. The other two came closer. Suddenly all fell silent. For there, in the other wing, the lights still blazed in old Aakerholm's chambers.

"It is just as if he were still there," said the doctor.

"Come—let us go!" exclaimed Krag. He led the way through the ancient manor's many rooms. The others followed close behind.

At last, they stood before the dead man's apartment and Krag started to try the keys.

No one spoke. It was so silent all around them that the doctor could hear his own heartbeat.

But suddenly Krag looked at Bengt and said: "I think that we two, Bengt, have an idea what we shall find in the three rooms."

The lock clicked. Krag had found the right key.

CHAPTER 6

The Third Room

The gentlemen stepped into the first room. There was nothing remotely peculiar about it, other than that it was furnished in accordance with the dead man's somewhat idiosyncratic tastes. A large variety of weapons hung on the walls, mainly rifles and revolvers. The next room was decorated in similar fashion.

"None of this is worth concealing," said the doctor.

"Several people have been in these rooms," Bengt answered. "For a long time, the old man had a deaf-mute servant who slept here in the first room."

Asbjørn Krag was opening the door to the innermost room, but stopped, his attention caught by Bengt's words.

"What did you say? A deaf-mute servant? That's odd."

"Yes, but the old man knew him from America. Apparently he had American Indian blood and he was very fond of his master. He is dead now."

Krag opened the door to the innermost room.

It was a large, beautifully appointed room. Over in one corner, behind a Japanese screen, stood Aakerholm's bed, which he always made up himself. The walls were hung with photographs and pictures, and were almost completely covered in tapestries and hangings besides, while the entire floor was carpeted with a thick, soft rug.

The three gentlemen stood for a while gazing curiously at the chairs, the table, the paintings, and the windows. The doctor was the first to speak.

"There is nothing remotely unusual here," he said.

"Well, I knew it from the start," Bengt interjected quickly. "That in the end all this secrecy with the three rooms was just one of the old man's eccentricities. After all, what could that dear old fellow have to hide?"

The doctor looked enquiringly at Asbjørn Krag.

"Shouldn't we examine the room more closely?"

"That will be quite unnecessary," replied Krag.

"I agree," said Bengt. "We'd best put out the lamps and get some sleep. We all need it after this terrible day."

Without paying the slightest attention to Bengt's remarks, Asbjørn Krag walked over to the wall and started to press and finger the tapestries and hangings that covered it.

All of a sudden, he murmured: "I thought as much, I thought as much."

And now, abruptly, he seemed to register Bengt's suggestion that they put out the lamps and leave, for he said. "No, of course we shan't leave. Ah, I can assure you gentlemen that this is a remarkable room. How full of foresight and wisdom the old man was."

"But what is the secret?" Bengt and the doctor chorused.

"That you will learn later, gentlemen. But for now, be so good as to assist me with a little experiment."

"Experiment?"

"No questions," Krag interrupted the doctor. "Just do as I say. My dear Doctor, could you repeat these few words for me? 'Take that, you devil!'"

"Take that, you devil," repeated the doctor, bewildered.

But Bengt remained silent. He had turned abruptly pale on hearing Asbjørn Krag's words, and now he looked at the detective with hate-filled eyes. Krag pretended not to notice.

"Louder," he continued, speaking to the doctor. "Much louder. You must shout it out. Imagine that one man is in the process of killing another. Just as he is about to crush his head in fury, say, he cries out: 'Take that, you devil!'"

The doctor repeated the cry, louder this time, and the detective declared himself satisfied.

"Now just wait here for two minutes," he said. "When precisely two minutes have passed, shout out those words."

With that, the detective left the room.

The doctor didn't have the faintest idea what was going on, but he decided to follow Krag's instructions down to the very last detail. He couldn't deny that a chill of unease swept over him when Krag left and he found himself alone with Bengt in this mysterious room, which had so violently stimulated his imagination.

Asbjørn Krag had gone through the rooms, across a corridor and through the parlour; there, in the pale light of the moon, he glimpsed the dead man beneath the white sheet. At last he came out into the courtyard and followed the same route he had taken the previous night, when he sought to spy on the old man and heard the cry.

He stopped beneath the three rooms and listened. Now the two minutes should have passed. He listened intently.

And there at last it came, the cry. The detective heard it clearly, but it seemed to come from some infinitely remote place, as if borne on a breath from another realm.

He went straight back to Aakerholm's room, where the doctor and Bengt awaited him.

"Are we quite finished now?" asked Bengt.

"Yes, thank you. I am fully satisfied with my examination of the rooms. But now we shall go down into the grounds."

"The grounds? And what shall we do there?"

"Examine the place where the Swissman found the body."

"Is that really necessary?"

"Absolutely. It is vital for us doctors to familiarize ourselves with every detail in a case like this."

Krag locked the doors behind them. He was the last person to leave the three rooms.

"Fetch the Swissman and a couple of other manservants," he ordered. "We must have some lanterns too."

Asbjørn Krag seemed determined to have his own way, to do as he pleased. He didn't pay the slightest attention to Bengt and ignored all his comments. Without further ado, he slipped the dead man's keys into his own pocket, even though it would have been more natural for them to be in Bengt's care. The doctor watched with pleasure as the detective's interest and eagerness grew with every passing half-hour; the very notion of tiredness seemed alien to him. The doctor realized that he was following a trail; but as to where it might lead, the doctor had not the faintest idea.

Andresen, the stable boy and another man had arrived in the meantime. All were carrying lanterns. Asbjørn Krag went up to his room for a moment, returning with his police lantern. It was a miraculous little device—an electric dark lantern that shone bright and strong as the clearest daylight.

Bengt's surprise intensified when he saw Krag in possession of this lantern. "A revolver and a dark lantern," he said, with a short, scornful laugh. "All you need to complete your equipment is a police badge."

By the entranceway two snorting horses stood harnessed to a sleigh. The coachman tramped back and forth beside it slapping his arms for warmth

Asbjørn Krag gave him a message and thrust a slip of paper into his hand.

"To the telegraph station, as quickly as possible. Wake up the clerk and have him send this message as an express telegram."

Minutes later, the sledge glided off to the town. At the same time, Krag, the doctor and Bengt set off into the grounds with Andresen and the other manservants. It was so cold that the snow creaked. The beam of the dangling lantern cast ghostly shafts of light in among the tree trunks.

"Here it is," said Andresen in his rough bass tones. The party halted and the Swissman shone his lantern at one of the nearby trees.

The tree was some four or five yards from the road.

Krag told the others to go back to the road. Then he shone his own lantern at the foot of the tree. There he found marks in the snow, which clearly indicated that a man had lain here recently.

Krag read the imprint as another man might read a book.

"He fell forward, face down in the snow," he said.

"Quite so," replied the Swissman.

"The right hand holding the revolver was trapped beneath him. He fell on top of it. But he threw his left hand over his head: I can see the distinct marks of all five fingers in the snow."

"Absolutely right."

"Look, there are some bloodstains here, too. But there cannot have been much blood. He must have died almost instantaneously. When was it you found him?"

"Roughly ten past eleven."

"Just when there was the most marvellous moonlight…"

Suddenly Krag gave a start. He had found new tracks in the snow.

"Wasn't Aakerholm wearing deerskin boots?"

"Yes."

"So what I am seeing here are his footprints. They start

76

by the road. He stepped off the road as one steps aside for an automobile—suddenly and very hastily. And then—aha! Now I see it. He walked the seven or eight steps over to the tree backwards."

Bengt had observed Krag's labours with increasing interest. Now he said: "It is hardly surprising the poor wretch backed away from the road to the tree. Naturally, he was afraid that someone might follow him and prevent him from pursuing the course of action he was planning."

"I did not say that it was striking or odd," Krag replied. "The main point for me is to note the fact."

He spent another quarter of an hour rooting around in the snow like a bloodhound. Then he switched off his lantern and said his work was complete.

The whole party returned to the manor.

Asbjørn Krag asked where the little avenue was and the Swissman showed him the way.

"This is the avenue that leads to the Silken Girl's home?" he asked.

"Yes, it leads to Widow Hjelm's villa," Bengt answered.

"Good. So at ten-thirty, Aakerholm is seen walking along the avenue. At ten past eleven, his body is found in the park—on the opposite side of the grounds, in other words. Is it possible for a man to make it from here to the Hjelm villa and back again to the part of the grounds where Aakerholm met his end in forty minutes?

The Swissman gave this some thought.

"It is possible," he said. "But I can't say for sure. At any

77

rate he would have had to walk very briskly."

"Well, we shall have to look into that tomorrow. It is already three-thirty now and the clouds will soon cover the moon. In a few minutes, the dark will prevent any further work, so we may as well go to bed."

Krag took the doctor by the arm, said a brief but friendly farewell to Bengt and stomped up the steps.

It was cosy and warm in the two guest rooms, and a fire crackled cheerily in the fireplace. It was not long before the cigars were lit.

At first, Krag was silent and meditative. For his part, the doctor was overwhelmed by the experiences of the past few hours. He sat a while with his head in his hands, then murmured: "I guessed as much, I guessed as much," adding with a shudder: "That fine old gentleman—and such a horrible death."

Suddenly he turned to Krag, who had already sunk back into his favourite spot: half-buried in an armchair, legs stretched towards the fireplace, the cigar in his mouth emitting clouds of smoke.

"Yesterday," he said, "you claimed to know the secret of the three rooms. But there was no secret."

From the depths of his armchair, Krag laughed aloud.

"Oh, the blindness of men," he said. "Of course those three rooms contain a secret. I guessed it at once in Kristiania when you told me of the old man's arrangements. Yesterday, the scales suddenly fell from my eyes and I became even more confident that I was correct when I heard about the deaf-mute servant—and now I am certain."

"But you barely heard anything about the deaf-mute servant," the doctor objected.

"Oh, I did though," answered Krag. "I heard that he was a deaf-mute. That was enough for me."

There was a brief lull in the conversation, during which fresh clouds of smoke billowed up from Krag's armchair. Then the doctor asked in a hesitant near-whisper: "Do you believe there is some mystery to Aakerholm's suicide?"

Krag laughed again.

"Suicide," he said. "That was no suicide. Aakerholm was murdered."

"Murdered?"

"Yes. Shot through the heart. Shot down like an old dog."

The doctor leaped up in horror.

"You say it so calmly," he cried. "But who in God's name is the murderer?"

"That I do not know. I do not yet know what he looks like. The only person who could have told me that, the old man himself, would not do so when I asked him yesterday."

"Who do you mean?"

"I mean the man the old chap saw by the pavilion. That is the murderer."

"And why wouldn't Aakerholm describe him to you?"

"Ha! That is another of the secrets of the three rooms."

The doctor paced back and forth feverishly.

"Murder," he muttered. "What a horrible notion!"

Suddenly he halted and said: "But those two shots,

Krag. There were only two shots and both barrels in Aakerholm's pistol had been fired."

"Those two shots," answered Krag, "are precisely what prove that this must have been a murder."

"I don't understand."

"Come now, it is perfectly obvious. The first shot was Aakerholm's. The second—fatal—shot was the murderer's. Aakerholm fired the first shot, at the murderer. You mustn't forget that Aakerholm had demonstrated his pistol skills earlier that evening by hitting the ace on the playing card. That meant only one of the pistol's barrels still contained a bullet."

The doctor stopped dead.

"You're absolutely right," he said. "You've convinced me."

"Besides," Krag continued. "The tracks in the wood show that Aakerholm must have seen the murderer appear before him on the road. He backed out into the snow immediately; perhaps he fired his shot at once but missed—and in this instance, it seems reasonable to me that he might miss, since he was almost certainly in a state of the most abject terror. Do you not recall the hideous expression on the murdered man's face?"

The doctor nodded.

"Well, then. After firing his pistol, he backed a few steps in towards the trees. Then he was struck by the fatal bullet."

The doctor sat for a long time, pondering.

"But I don't understand," he said at last. "Why would Aakerholm go out into the grounds in the middle of the night.

"I do not understand that either," Asbjørn Krag answered as he lit a third cigar. "But the Silken Girl must certainly be able to tell us. Do not forget, doctor, that we have yet to speak to one of the main characters in this drama: the beautiful widow."

CHAPTER 7

PAGE 248

Asbjørn Krag and the doctor sat talking for almost another hour. The detective did not want to retire for the night until he had heard from the telegraph office.

At last, he heard the jingling of sleigh-bells far down the road. It was the coachman returning. As he turned into the courtyard, Asbjørn Krag waved him over.

Two telegrams had arrived: one from Kristiania and the other from America.

Krag read the latter missive attentively and the expression on his face told the doctor that the contents of the telegrams did not displease him.

But now the doctor was tired. It was increasingly difficult for him to keep his heavy eyelids open. The terrible tension of the past days had taken too great a toll on him. So he stood up and left his detective friend with a hearty goodnight.

But Asbjørn Krag was still as lively and alert as ever in both body and mind. No sooner had the doctor gone to bed than Krag took the box containing the fragments of mirror out of his wardrobe. He laid them out carefully on the floor, upside down. Then he tried to put the pieces together. At first, he failed, but he laboured away, steadily feeling his way forward. At length, he had restored almost half of the mirror.

As his work progressed, Krag became ever more satisfied and when once the pieces had begun to fit together, the pace of his work picked up. By the end, he confirmed what he had hoped to find: In one corner of the mirror, a perfect square of mercury had been scraped off the glass. It had been done recently.

"Now all I need to know," the detective murmured as he collected all the fragments into a pile again, "is what the old man was made to see in this square. I imagine it must have been some terrifying word of accusation."

When Krag was finished with the mirror, he took out the little book he had snatched up the previous evening. From his vantage point, he had seen how feverishly Aakerholm leafed through it to find some very particular thing. Krag could not see the page numbers, but he estimated that Aakerholm had stopped at last at a place between pages 200 and 250. Krag therefore began reading from page 200, checking every single word. The book was in English and appeared to be a highly entertaining novel of the lighter sort, but Krag noted neither the plot nor the entertainment the book offered: his concern was to find a hidden meaning in what he read. For a long time, it escaped him. There was no single word, no sentence that he could reasonably construe to be connected with the matter in hand. But he found it at last: at the bottom of page 248, he found some lines. An exclamation by one of the characters in the book. It seemed to Krag that these two lines stood out, isolated and crying out for attention, so clear was their connection to the events with which he was currently engaged.

Asbjørn Krag hid the book in his holdall. Now he would rest for an hour or two. But before getting into bed, he opened the window to let in a breath of fresh night air. The night was still clear and cold. The moonlight bathed the landscape, painting the snow a glittering white, the houses and patches of forest dark and blueish, and all the shadows black as coal. Here and there, life was beginning to stir out on some distant road or in some isolated cottage. The manor itself lay silent and still, the ancient parkland girdling it like a broad black belt. Krag noticed that the light still shone in Bengt's windows. Other than that, all the lights in the great estate were out and no sound of life or humanity was to be heard.

The detective shut the window and closed the curtains. Then he checked to see that his door was shut, took out his little black box and placed one of the gold-plated revolvers on the table. The instant he lay down, all his thoughts and ponderings about the case were seemingly expelled from his brain. He slept at once.

* * *

By ten the next morning, Asbjørn Krag was at the home of Widow Hjelm, the Silken Girl. She had already heard about the death, which had—as she told Krag at once—grieved her deeply.

As the doctor attending the deceased on his final day, Krag said, he saw it as his duty to obtain any information that might help explain why Aakerholm had resorted to this desperate deed.

"It is as unbelievable to me as to you," answered the widow. Krag asked whether she had noticed anything odd about Aakerholm's behaviour lately.

"He did behave very strangely the past few days," she replied. "I do not know what was wrong, but at any rate to the best of my knowledge, he was not toying with any notions of suicide."

"When were you to marry?"

It was clear to Krag that his question was unwelcome to the widow and that it pained her to speak of the matter, but after a moment's thought, she answered.

"We were to be married in a month. Aakerholm was always pressing for haste."

"Why?"

"I really don't know. But—especially recently—he often spoke of bringing forward the date of our wedding. He said it was important."

"Do you know Aakerholm's adopted son?"

"Young Bengt? Yes, I know him."

"What was his attitude to the relationship between you and Aakerholm?"

"He did not like it. He opposed it with all his might."

"Does it seem feasible to you that his behaviour might have been the cause of Aakerholm's severe despondency over the past few weeks?"

The widow answered evasively. "Aakerholm was not always despondent. He had many light-hearted moments."

"You haven't answered my question."

She had become somewhat uneasy and after thinking a while, she said: "Aakerholm often spoke bitterly of his adopted son. I believe Bengt's stubborn opposition was the reason why he was in such a hurry to get married."

"Was Aakerholm afraid of his son, then?"

"Oh no, not in the least—but I had the impression that he was afraid of something else."

"Something else?"

"He spoke a great deal lately about an event in his life that might end up casting a shadow over his old age."

"Did he say anything about the nature of this event?"

"No, but he did say it was a very serious matter."

"Did you not press him to tell you more?"

"Of course."

"What did he say to that?"

"That I would be taken into his confidence one day."

"That he would tell you everything, in other words?"

"Yes."

"But when?"

The widow began to pace nervously to and fro across the room. "Well, that is precisely what is so peculiar."

"Ah?"

"I was expecting Aakerholm here yesterday night."

"At eleven o'clock," Krag added.

"Yes. But how could you possibly know that?"

"Was that when he was to tell you his dread secret?"

"Yes, he had promised me he would. But then he never came."

"Well, I can assure you, Madame, that he had every intention of doing so."

"Truly? But didn't he die at eleven o'clock?"

"At eleven-ten, yes. But at ten-thirty, he left the manor to come and meet you. He was seen in the little avenue."

"Ah, yes—in that case he was almost certainly on his way to me."

"And when he left the manor," Krag continued, "he almost certainly had no intention of taking his own life. So it seems that something must have happened to him, something unexpected, between ten-thirty and eleven o'clock. And it must have happened in the avenue."

"People hardly use it as a rule," said the widow. "But tell me—since you appear to know everything: Where was Bengt at this time?"

"He was with me at the club. We were both called back to Kvamberg when Aakerholm's death was discovered."

"It is all most peculiar," said the widow. "I find the whole thing quite incomprehensible."

"Does it seem likely to you that Aakerholm could suddenly have been overwhelmed by thoughts of suicide while on his way to you, turned back, walked into the grounds and shot himself?"

"No, it seems impossible to me. Something must have happened to him."

"You are quite right," said Krag. "Something did happen to him."

"What do you think it could be?"

"I believe he met someone."

"In the avenue?"

"Yes."

The widow pondered this. Krag noticed that she was growing uneasy.

"Who on earth could it have been?" she asked.

Krag looked at her. She shuddered and a half-terrified, half-imploring expression came over her face.

"Won't you explain it to me?" she said.

"Yes, I shall, as soon as I hear who this person was—who it was that Aakerholm met yesterday evening when he was on his way to see you."

"How could I know that?"

"You do know it. For the man he met in that little avenue, which is otherwise unused, came from your house."

"That is impossible. No one has been here."

"Listen now, Madam," Krag said urgently. "Were you fond of Aakerholm?"

"I liked him a great deal. He was a fine old man."

It did not escape Krag's notice that she glanced uneasily at the door when she spoke, as if expecting someone to enter.

Krag continued. "But Aakerholm had enemies, who ultimately drove him to his death."

"So I am beginning to understand," she said.

"Will you help me by unmasking his enemies?"

The widow walked straight up to him and held out a hand.

"I will," she said in a heartfelt tone.

Krag saw that she meant it in earnest.

But suddenly she gave a start. Krag heard a noise in the hallway—somebody had arrived. The widow made to run towards the door but Krag swiftly grasped her hand and held it tight. She seemed about to scream, but just then the door opened and a man stepped in.

It was Bengt.

This was not the person Krag had expected to see and he realized from the widow's cry of surprise that she had not been expecting Bengt either.

Bengt was the first to speak.

"You, here?" he said. "You are a peculiar man, sir."

In an instant Krag had regained his customary composure.

"Surely," he replied, "you would give me leave to pay a farewell visit to an acquaintance. I was a good friend of Widow Hjelm's late husband."

As he said this, he looked at the widow, who answered quickly, despite her bewilderment; "Yes, indeed. It has been a pleasure to see you."

"So you leave today?" asked Bengt.

"I shall leave in two hours."

"And you are satisfied with your investigations, I presume?"

"I am satisfied. I have found what I was looking for."

The tone of Asbjørn Krag's voice caused Bengt to knit his brows.

CHAPTER 8

THE SILKEN GIRL

As Asbjørn Krag walked down the little avenue, a multitude of thoughts tumbled around in his mind. His conversation with the widow had largely confirmed his suspicions. But new and unexpected questions had arisen. What did Bengt want with the Silken Girl? She had clearly been as surprised as the detective by the adopted son's sudden arrival.

While he walked along the avenue deep in thought, he heard someone hurrying after him. The detective turned around and saw a young man. Krag stopped.

"Are you looking for me?" he asked, when the man was close enough.

"Yes, I am," the man replied. "I have a message for you."

"From whom?"

"From Mrs Hjelm. I'm her stable boy."

The man looked around as if afraid someone might be spying on them.

"I have a letter," he whispered. "I am to ask you to read it and then answer yes or no."

Krag seized the little white envelope that gleamed in

the man's hand. On opening it, he found a card. Written in haste in a fine female hand, it said: "I must, simply must speak to you before you leave."

There was no signature.

"Well?" asked the man tensely.

"You are perhaps aware of the contents of the note?" Krag responded.

"No, I'm not."

"Did you see your mistress write it?"

"Yes. She called me into the front parlour and wrote it while I waited."

"Was she alone?"

"Yes, but young Aakerholm was in the next room."

"Good. You may send your mistress my regards and say that I shall do as she asks."

The man said farewell and made to run back to the villa but Asbjørn Krag stopped him.

"Listen here," he said. "Where does he live—the man who paid Mrs Hjelm a visit yesterday evening and left the villa a few minutes before eleven?"

The man seemed somewhat surprised by the question but replied:

"I don't know."

Krag smiled to see how well his simple ruse had worked.

"Ah, well," he said. "It may be of no consequence. My regards to Mrs Hjelm."

And with that, the detective continued on his way.

When he returned to Kvamberg, he met the doctor out

in the courtyard. The doctor seemed slightly agitated.

"I must speak to you right away," he said.

The two gentlemen went up to their rooms.

The doctor shut the door and stood in an attitude that suggested he had an important message to convey.

"Something happened while you were out—something unexpected."

"Have they found the man from the pavilion?" Krag answered in a tone of the most utter indifference.

"No."

"What has happened then?"

"The police have paid a visit."

"Really."

"An inspector and two constables. A formal investigation into Aakerholm's death has been opened."

"Good," Krag said, as he sat down calmly in his customary spot by the fireplace.

"Why, you are not in the least bit surprised!" cried the doctor.

"No," answered Asbjørn Krag. "I am only surprised by the unexpected, Doctor, and this event can hardly be called unexpected, since I myself set it in motion."

"You?"

"Yes. I had to involve the local police to a certain extent at this stage, to prevent anyone from moving the body. Now, of course, this has been forbidden."

"Yes, I heard the Swissman say as much."

"Then everything is in order."

"What are you planning to do yourself?" the doctor asked impatiently.

"I am leaving."

"No! What on earth do you mean?"

"I will be leaving this very morning. My suitcase is packed."

"When will you return?"

"Tonight. But no one must know that."

"Ah, now I begin to understand. You want to lull Bengt into a false sense of security. When he believes you to be far away you will actually be close at hand observing him."

"Precisely. I will return here tonight at eleven o'clock precisely. You must ensure that I am able to steal in unseen. Your bedroom window overlooks the park. Make sure it is darkened at eleven, but sit by the window and observe what happens. Have a rope to hand. Then leave the rest to me."

"All this shall be done," the doctor said. "I am most curious," he continued. "What came of your conversation with the widow?"

"Not a great deal."

"Does she have anything to do with this drama?"

"We shall have to wait and see. I have at any rate established how the murder was committed."

The doctor was sitting directly opposite Krag. He looked at the detective with a penetrating gaze and said: "I shall not be kept out of this. Tell me—how *was* the murder committed?"

Krag smiled.

"I'll gladly tell you," he answered. "It is quite simple and straightforward: No sooner had Bengt and I been driven to the club than Aakerholm hurried to visit his wife-to-be, the Silken Girl—properly known as Mrs Hjelm. They had agreed that he would meet her at eleven o'clock on the dot. Aakerholm had promised that he would tell her his dread secret."

"What dread secret?" the doctor asked.

"The secret that is inextricably linked to the three rooms. Well, then, as he was about to leave, he happened to find his old pistol on the table in the parlour, where he had left it after his fine sharp shooting. He thrust it in his pocket without any notion that he might need to have it on his person or might have some call for it. Then he left the house and set off down the avenue. All this we know, don't we?"

The doctor nodded.

"Despite the moonlight, the avenue was very dark that evening," Krag continued. "Based on the facts I have now gathered, I can describe pretty clearly what happened. I think Aakerholm was some two-thirds of the way along the avenue, and had reached roughly the point where he would be able to catch a glimpse of Mrs Hjelm's villa. Precisely the point where the avenue curves around a steepish hillock. There he came to a halt when he saw the villa's veranda door open and a gentleman step out."

"Out of Mrs Hjelm's villa?"

"Yes. It goes without saying that Aakerholm was surprised by this. He surely wondered who this gentleman could be. Wishing to establish his identity, he quickly hid behind the hillock, for he did not wish to be seen himself. From then on, events unfolded rapidly and the tragedy played out within a matter of minutes. The stranger walked past Aakerholm, who was unable to recognize him in the darkness. He waited until the stranger had walked some way further, then followed him. The stranger walked along the entire avenue and now Aakerholm naturally assumed that he would turn to the right, onto the main road. But what actually happened? The stranger turned right and walked into Aakerholm's own grounds, taking precisely the broad path that passes right by the demolished pavilion and ends in a forest on the other side. At this point, Aakerholm must have thought that if he was to discover the stranger's identity, he must head him off. It is clear that he must have run, taking a short cut that would allow him to approach the stranger face to face. I'm sure you'll agree that this is as plain as day?"

"Absolutely," said the doctor. "Do go on."

"In this way, Aakerholm is able to see the stranger's face. And when he sees who it is, he seizes his pistol at once and fires it at him. But the old man has been overcome by such terror that his hand trembles and he misses—or at least wounds the other man only slightly."

The doctor interrupted.

"Well, now you've lost me," he said. "I don't see why it was necessary for Aakerholm to shoot the other man."

"He certainly had to when he saw who the stranger was."

"Who in heaven's name was he?"

"None other than the man from the pavilion of course."

"Ah, now I follow."

Krag continued.

"After firing his one shot, the old man—reeling in terror, unarmed and helpless—staggered a few steps backwards. And that's when the other man shot him down in cold blood."

The doctor got up, evidently much disturbed.

"That is how it must have happened," he said. "I see it all clearly now. But the important thing now is to track down this stranger, this mysterious murderer who walks among us."

"Quite right," Krag responded. "He is the person we must track down. He may well betray himself tonight, when he believes me to be far away from the manor."

"Yes, but how will you get back in?"

"I will get off at one of the nearby stations en route, then make my way here on a fast horse. I have promised to meet the widow tomorrow afternoon and I will most certainly obtain some vital information from her. After that, we shall see whether I don't manage to collar that stranger within the next twenty-four hours; that mysterious man who was the first to discover the secret of the three rooms, who then inspired such terrible fear in Aakerholm and who, at last, fired a bullet through the venerable old gentleman's heart."

Asbjørn Krag had barely finished speaking before there was a knock at the door.

Bengt came in.

Krag saw at once that he was seething with indignation. There were red patches on his cheeks and he fixed Krag with a hateful gaze.

"Is it true that you are leaving?" Bengt asked.

"Yes."

"Straight away?"

"A train leaves Kvamberg station in an hour. I plan to be on it."

"I have some good advice for you," Bengt said. "You should take the express, which will leave town shortly. It is much more comfortable and stops at no other stations along the way."

Krag realized at once that Bengt suspected he did not wish to leave. If Krag took the express, Bengt could be certain that he would end up many dozens of miles away from the Kvamberg district.

"Good," he said. "Thank you for your advice. I will gladly take the express."

"Very well, but before you travel, I have a complaint to make."

"How may I be of service?"

"You have interfered in my affairs in the most intolerable fashion."

"Is that so?"

"Indeed. For you were certainly the person who arranged for the police to come here and start rooting around in the old man's suicide. Is this business not tragic enough in itself without also bringing scandal upon the family?"

"The family?"

"As his adopted son, I have the right to use that expression. What's more, you have insulted one of my friends?"

"Dare I ask whom?"

"The police inspector."

"Ah, Polis—the fat drunkard I met at the club."

"Perhaps you failed to hear that me call him my friend. Somehow, inexplicably, you have managed to ensure that not he but some green deputy police inspector has been entrusted with the case. I don't know how you swung it, but a telegram was apparently sent from the Department of Justice in Kristiania."

The doctor, who had been listening to the conversation with growing astonishment, immediately realized that this explained the telegraphing Krag had done the night before.

Asbjørn Krag replied: "Do you genuinely think I did all this?"

"Yes."

"Then you are a simpleton to tell me so."

Krag looked at his watch.

"I had best be leaving," he said, "if I'm to have any hope of making the express. I imagine you have already been kind enough to arrange a sleigh for me."

"The sleigh is ready harnessed."

The three gentlemen walked down to the courtyard.

Just by the main entrance stood the young deputy inspector to whom Bengt had so scornfully referred. He was a lively little chap with an intelligent face and a pair of shrewd eyes. When he spied Asbjørn Krag, he seemed surprised and greeted him with considerable respect. Bengt, startled, noticed this.

"Ah, are you here?" Krag said. "What a pleasure to see you again. I seem to recall I once treated you for a sore throat. How is your health these days?"

The policeman, who understood at once, quickly replied: "Excellent, thank you, Doctor. I am in the best of health."

"Well," said Krag, placing a particular emphasis on the words, "ailments of that nature are quickly cured if one is only careful enough."

"Which I am, Doctor."

"Excellent. Goodbye."

"Goodbye, Doctor."

As Krag stepped into the sleigh, the young policeman turned away, a peculiar smile creeping over his face.

CHAPTER 9

THE REDHEAD

When Asbjørn Krag had settled comfortably in the sledge, Bengt asked him: "In our family we have a custom of always accompanying our guests beyond the door. I hope you will permit me to travel with you." His sweet smile failed to mask the bitterness on his face.

"But of course," Krag said. "It will be a pleasure to have such congenial company."

Bengt got into the sleigh, Krag said farewell to the doctor and the police officer once more, and then the sleigh glided through the gates of the estate and on down the road, the fine steeds steaming between the carriage shafts.

On the way to town, Bengt was reserved and grave. Krag, by contrast, was extremely talkative. He expounded on how splendid it was that the police had become involved. It would spare the family any gossip later. Old Aakerholm had, after all, died under very mysterious circumstances, and gossip has a way of adding and subtracting from the truth—and that was why it was so splendid that the police... etc. Bengt answered rarely and then only in monosyllables. But then Asbjørn Krag began to talk about

Bengt himself. He was after all an ambitious young man—and rich to boot; should he not be looking about for a wife? Krag hinted that Bengt might pay court to Widow Hjelm. He had observed Bengt's eyes that morning; they looked precisely like the eyes of a man in love. It could be a fine match and as a matter of fact the old man's death was rather convenient, really.

Bengt turned away from him disdainfully, muttering, "Lord, what an oaf."

But Krag was secretly enjoying this comedy. Above all because he had managed to pull the wool over Bengt's eyes once again.

The sledge glided to a stop in front of the little town's railway station.

"If you should ever find yourself in Kristiania," Krag said, "I would very much appreciate a visit from you. I will try to repay you for the interesting hours I have spent on your estate."

"Interesting!" cried Bengt, staring at the detective in surprise. "As far as I'm concerned, these past few days have been quite dreadful, by God!"

"Now, now," Krag said, attempting to pat the other man on the shoulder—an amiable overture that Bengt pointedly repulsed. "When I say interesting, I mean of course that it has been interesting for me to observe this case of the old man's illness and death from a professional point of view."

Bengt turned away from him indignantly.

"And now," concluded Krag, "I must entrust my precious life to the express. It leaves in barely a minute."

Bengt looked as if he were fervently hoping for a fatal derailment, but he said: "Just to be on the safe side, I shall make contact with the local railway stations to check that no accident happens to befall you or the train."

Krag realized at once that Bengt intended to prevent him from arranging for the train to stop at any of the stations along the way. But he pretended to be oblivious, greeting Bengt's words with laughter as if this were an excellent joke. Then he shook Bengt warmly by the hand and asked him to send his regards to the doctor and everyone else at the manor.

After the train had set off, Krag appeared in one of the windows and nodded enthusiastically at Bengt, who quickly turned his back on him.

Asbjørn Krag remained by the window, observing the landscape that glided past him. The cheerful expression had left his face. He stared gravely towards Kvamberg, whose white facade he could spy far off on the horizon. All of a sudden the little station at Kvamberg waltzed by; ten minutes later, the express passed through another station. It was now a fifteen-minute journey to the next.

Krag looked at his watch. Not for an instant did he have the faintest shadow of a doubt about how to proceed. When a further five minutes had passed and the train was speeding across a flat plain, the detective reached out a hand and quickly tugged the emergency brake. At once, the train began to slow.

Krag's action provoked considerable dismay in the compartment. Passengers came running from other compartments eager to find out what the problem was. Had there been an accident? Had he fallen ill?

With almost perfect composure, Krag replied that nothing at all had happened; he merely wished to alight from the train. As he spoke, the train stopped and, to his fellow-passengers' considerable and approving amusement, Krag began to gather up his effects—his holdall, his little black box and his fur coat. A pipe-smoking English winter tourist who had observed this scene with the utmost gravity and in complete silence, got up, shook Krag's hand, muttered "Jolly good show" and then sat back down again.

But just then a pair of conductors came rushing into the carriage in a terrible fright.

"Who pulled the emergency brake?" they asked, speaking over each other.

"I did," said Krag as he attempted to push past them.

"Why?" asked the conductors.

"Because I am getting off here."

The passengers laughed. The conductors tried to stop Krag.

"That is a serious breach of regulations," one of them said. "You'll be getting a very stiff fine."

"Nonetheless," Krag answered, as he gave his address in Kristiania. "I need to get off here."

The passengers laughed again. But now the conductors had become really angry.

"We won't let you off!" they shouted. "When the train gets to Kristiania, we'll have you arrested."

Instead of answering, Krag pulled down the window and swiftly threw his effects out onto the snow: first his fur coat, then the holdall and then the little black box. After that, he measured his opponents from top to toe with his gaze, then clenched his fists with a scornful laugh. His powerful muscles rippled visibly beneath the sleeves of his jacket.

"Jolly good show," murmured the winter tourist approvingly, taking another puff on his shag pipe.

But the conductors reluctantly stepped aside for Asbjørn Krag, who rushed past them and, with a single bound, was out in the snow with his things. An instant later, he was over the fence and standing on the country road. In a mocking voice, he shouted to the conductors: "You'd best be on your way. Express trains are meant to be fast, are they not?"

And there was nothing for it but to set the train in motion again. When it left, every window was crowded with happy, smiling faces and waving handkerchiefs. But the conductors swore that their revenge would cost Krag dear.

"Well, that is how it goes," Asbjørn Krag muttered to himself, "when one cannot reveal one's true identity as a policeman."

He walked to the nearest decent-sized farm, where he borrowed a warm sleigh and a splendid horse. The prospect of the last—and weightiest—part of his assignment had put Krag in excellent spirits.

After a three- or four-hour drive, he was back in the district of Kvamberg. He alighted from the sleigh in the vicinity of Widow Hjelm's villa and instructed the lad who had driven the sleigh to return to his farm as fast as he could, without stopping or speaking to anyone along the way. The lad gave his word, beaming with goodwill when he saw the generous tip he'd been given, and drove off.

Before going into the villa, Krag ascertained that the widow was alone. When he entered her room, he realised that she had been expecting him. She was more nervous than on the previous day and it was clear to Krag that she had been crying.

"I beg your pardon for my behaviour yesterday," she began. "But the information you gave me and the questions you asked caught me entirely off guard. It was rash of me to try and hide anything from you, and I regretted it the moment you left. That is why I sent my man after you."

"I realised that," Krag answered. "Will you tell me the purpose of Bengt's visit?"

"I can assure you it was entirely unexpected."

"I could see that."

"He visited me because he wished to inform me of his father's death."

"Then we may now proceed. Who was the gentleman who left your villa at around eleven o'clock yesterday night, and whom old Aakerholm met in the avenue?"

Widow Hjelm had to stifle some powerful emotion before she could respond.

"You can trust me implicitly," Krag said.

"I am certain of that," the lady answered. "And nor do I have anything to conceal. As you may have heard," she continued, "I travelled abroad fairly extensively both during my husband's lifetime and after his death. I adored travel and may, perhaps, have lived somewhat more freely abroad than my reputation at home could have borne. I have gambled in both Ostend and Monte Carlo."

"And lost?"

"I won some substantial amounts, but lost most of it. Now, if you are an intelligent soul, you will realise that a person—especially a woman—in thrall to a passion for gambling is not especially particular about the connections she makes, as long as these connections lead her to the roulette table. On one occasion, I found myself in an embarrassing situation in Monte Carlo, and was assisted by a man whose price has since proved high. I soon discovered what kind of a man he was: a professional gambler and a swindler, who always had the police on his trail. As soon as I realised this, I at once left the town and the country where he was. But he followed me and I only narrowly escaped being found. Only once I had settled here at home did I feel safe. But then—can you imagine my horror?—he suddenly turned up here in the district. He started to threaten me and ordered me to call off my marriage to Aakerholm. But I decided then that there must be an end to this torment and refused. Yesterday night was the last time he came to my home. The encounter ended in a terrible scene and he left me in a rage after swearing revenge. The time was eleven o'clock and that is the man Aakerholm met. It pains me greatly to think that the sight of this man leaving my home may be the reason why Aakerholm…"

Overcome by emotion, she could speak no more.

Krag asked: "What is his name?"

"I know him by the name of Jim Charter."

"American?"

"Yes."

"How did he find out that you had come to Norway?"

"He didn't find it out at all. He told me the first time I met him here that he was just as surprised to meet me as I was to meet him."

At once, Asbjørn Krag became exceedingly alert and interested.

"I thought as much," he muttered. "What does this Jim Charter look like?"

"Tall, muscular, red beard, horrid grey eyes. He must be around forty years of age."

"Did he ever refer to his appearance?" Krag asked. "To his red hair for example."

The widow looked surprised.

"Why yes," she answered. "Now that you mention it, I distinctly remember him once saying that his appearance was worth a great deal of money."

The detective leapt up.

"Excellent!" he cried. "Now we have the final link in the chain."

"Whatever do you mean?"

"I am thinking of the three rooms."

"The three rooms?"

Krag moved closer to the widow, who stared at him, anxious and puzzled.

"Do you really believe that Aakerholm killed himself?" he asked.

"Well, should I not believe…"

"No, my dear lady; he was shot, murdered."

"Good heavens! Murdered? By whom?"

"By Jim Charter."

"I don't understand."

"You will soon do so, dear lady."

Widow Hjelm buried her face in her hands and sank into a chair sobbing. "Poor, wretched soul! But you will surely be avenged by the time day dawns!"

The doctor was sitting in his room at Kvamberg at around midnight awaiting the arrival of Asbjørn Krag. Everyone had gone to bed and total silence reigned over the manor.

The doctor opened the window overlooking the park and put out his lamp, the better to orient himself in the darkness outside.

A peculiar atmosphere settled over him as he sat there by the window staring out over the dark park where the hideous drama had played out barely twelve hours before.

He imagined he could see figures in disguise moving among the trees, but they were only the shadows of wind-tossed branches. The precise hour of Krag's return was nigh and—right on time—a human figure came stealing towards the manor.

It stopped beneath his window and the doctor heard a whistle.

He responded in kind, then threw out the rope, whose other end was bound tightly to the window ledge.

The doctor heard someone climbing up the rope. An instant later, the figure jumped through the window and into the room. The doctor quickly lit the lamp.

But then all the blood in his veins seemed to freeze to ice.

The person who had come in through the window was not Asbjørn Krag.

As his mind turned to Aakerholm's murderer and the mysterious man in the pavilion, the doctor felt a prickle of fear in his temples.

Before him stood the menacing figure of a tall, muscular man with a red beard.

CHAPTER 10

THE DEPUTY POLICE INSPECTOR

The red-bearded man stood still and stared at the doctor for almost a minute. And the doctor, horrified, backed towards the door.

"Stand still!" the man ordered, in a peculiar tone. His voice seemed to come from far away. Just then the doctor saw the glint of a revolver in his hand, and that stopped him in his tracks, although he was shuddering with terror. What did the stranger want—was he going to kill him? Surely it must be Asbjørn Krag he was after?

The doctor summoned up his courage and asked as sternly as he could manage under the circumstances: "How dare you force your way into my room like this?"

The man did not reply but fiddled casually with his revolver. His eyes had a peculiar sparkle.

"There are police officers in the house," the doctor continued. "If you do not remove yourself at once, I will summon them."

The man smiled. Suddenly he pointed the revolver at

the doctor; pointed it directly at his head, and then, in that peculiar voice that seemed to come from a great distance, he said: "Turn to face the fireplace at once, or you're a dead man."

The doctor hesitated.

"At once," the voice repeated.

There was nothing for it: he turned towards the fireplace. But a whisper of terror ran through him, for he could sense the little black muzzle of the revolver pointing straight at his neck.

He stood like this for roughly a minute. Then, all at once, he heard laughter behind him—familiar laughter. He quickly turned his head.

Asbjørn Krag sat laughing in the chair. On the table before him lay a red wig and a red beard.

So great was the doctor's surprise that he struggled a while to recover the power of speech. All the while, Krag laughed, revelling in the other's confusion.

At last the doctor said: "You nearly scared the life out of me, Krag. Don't you think that practical joke of yours was a bit beyond the pale?"

"But you knew I would return at eleven o'clock on the dot," the detective replied. "You knew that I must arrive in secret and in disguise. It was no joke."

"Thank heavens it was you. I thought it was the other man."

"Who?"

"Him, the murderer—the man from the pavilion."

"That wasn't such a bad guess on your part. When I'm wearing the wig and false beard, I really do look like him."

"Have you seen him then?"

"No, but the widow tells me so. She knows him."

"Ah, I see. Could she be an accomplice to the murder?"

"No, absolutely not. She is entirely uninvolved. But she does know the murderer."

"Is he still in the area?"

"Yes, and he is apparently in our very midst. Has anything suspicious happened?"

"No, nothing whatsoever. Bengt has spent almost all the time since your departure in his rooms."

"And the young deputy police inspector?"

"Well, he's certainly a peculiar fellow. On several occasions he literally hovered around me trying to strike up a conversation. It was almost as if he thought I had something to tell him."

Krag nodded.

"Hmmm. But you didn't tell him anything?"

"No. He, on the other hand, told me at one point that Bengt had now called all the local railway stations."

"And what did you say to that?"

"I didn't say anything in particular. I didn't really understand what he was getting at."

Krag nodded again and murmured to himself: "Ah yes, he certainly is a clever chap. Shhh."

The detective placed a finger on his lips and both men listened.

Out in the corridor, they could hear stealthy footsteps.

The doctor reached for the revolver, but Krag pushed him away.

"It's him," he said.

An instant later, a pattern of knocks came on the door and Krag called out "Come in."

It was the young deputy police inspector. He wasn't wearing his uniform and was carrying a dark lantern.

"That is excellent," said Krag. "Douse the lamp, doctor. Otherwise there will be too many shadows in here."

The doctor blew out the lamp. Now, the only light in the room was the broad white beam from the dark lantern, which spread across the floor.

"I got your note," whispered the deputy police inspector. "And I hope that I have arrived punctually."

"Excellent."

"Is it time to take action?"

"Not yet."

The three gentlemen sat in silence for a while. Then the deputy police inspector said: "I was very surprised to meet you here. But I realised at once that there was mischief brewing. That also explained the mysterious order from the Department of Justice in Kristiania."

"Yes, I didn't want to have that drunken old police inspector here," answered the detective.

"I'll say nothing on that score. How do things stand? I assume the old man was murdered."

"Yes, shot through the heart."

"I thought so. Was it Bengt?"

"No, he is merely the accomplice."

"So he mustn't get away either. He lives over there in that wing. He has spent the whole day looking at papers and correspondence."

The deputy police inspector went over to the window that overlooked the courtyard, which offered a view of both the three rooms and the windows of Bengt's apartment.

Asbjørn Krag and the doctor followed him.

"Shut the dark lantern," ordered the detective.

A moment later, the room was plunged into total darkness.

Asbjørn Krag rolled up the blind.

There was light in only two of Bengt's rooms. A shadow was visible, moving, against the curtain.

"It's Bengt," whispered the doctor.

"Yes, it must be," answered Krag.

They could tell from the shadow that Bengt was sitting at a table. Suddenly, the shadow made a movement with its hands that resembled a gesture.

"He is speaking to someone," the detective and the deputy police inspector said in unison.

The three gentlemen stared across at the illuminated windows. It became more and more evident that Bengt was in conversation with someone—another person who sat on behind the light.

But all of a sudden, Bengt jumped up and, as he did so, the shadow of the second person appeared on the curtain.

The detective could see that it was a tall, bearded man, wearing a fur hat and a hunting jacket, carrying a bag with a shoulder strap.

"Who on earth can that be?" asked the deputy police inspector.

"I shall tell you," replied the detective, seizing the other man's upper arm fiercely. "It is the murderer. It is the man who shot Aakerholm."

"Shouldn't we apprehend them? I have two constables in the servants' quarters, ready to dash out at a signal from me."

"Not yet."

The deputy police inspector heard a click and realised that Asbjørn Krag was checking his revolver in the darkness.

The shadows in Bengt's window now stood close together.

"They are saying their farewells," whispered the doctor.

The man in the hunting jacket turned and left the room. Bengt followed him, holding the lamp high in one hand. The three men saw each of the windows illuminated in succession as Bengt and his companion proceeded through the wing. In the end, the outer door was opened and a dark shadow stole out into the courtyard. Bengt returned to his rooms again with the lamp.

"Keep an eye on the one who is still here," whispered Asbjørn Krag. "Don't make any noise but give me your assurance that he will not leave the manor."

"Trust me. He…"

But Krag had already left the room. He tiptoed rapidly

down the stairs and along the corridor. As he came out into the courtyard, he saw the man in the hunting jacket disappearing into the dark grounds.

The detective glanced over at Bengt's apartment. No. The shadow was once again sitting calmly at a table.

Then Krag crept along the wall of the house, silent and supple as a cat. He blessed the recent thaw—the cold no longer nipped so bitterly at the soles of his shoes.

When Krag reached the grounds, he caught another glimpse of the dark shadow in front of him. He followed the man slowly, as soundlessly as he could.

The figure walked past the spot where Aakerholm had been murdered. There it stopped and looked to the side, but immediately moved on. Asbjørn Krag secretly admired the other man's cold-bloodedness.

The man with the hunting bag walked indifferently past the demolished pavilion, turned left and continued along one of the garden's narrowest paths. By now, Krag had nearly caught up with him.

Suddenly the man stopped by a ramshackle old summer house and looked around. The detective barely had time to hide behind a tree. The man opened a door, whose rusty hinges squealed horribly, and went into the summer house.

Krag waited for around five minutes but the man did not re-emerge. Then the detective muttered to himself: Well, well, Jim Charter, it will soon be time for us to have a chat.

He left his lookout post and ran back the same way he

nad come.

But instead of returning to the doctor's rooms, he walked across the courtyard and turned into the little avenue. He did not meet a living soul along the way.

Light was shining in several of the windows at Widow Hjelm's villa. Krag went straight up to the main entrance and knocked on the door.

The widow herself opened it.

"He hasn't arrived yet," she whispered.

"I know," replied Krag. "But he is probably not on my heels. Hurry up and shut the door."

When Krag had come inside and seen the widow's face, he said: "You must try to calm yourself. It seems he is very suspicious."

"I will compose myself as best I can," said the widow, "but you must admit that I have a peculiar encounter ahead of me. Look—here's a hiding place for you."

The widow showed the detective to one of the doors. Here, concealed behind some heavy curtains, he would be able to see and hear everything that happened in the room without himself being visible.

"Are you armed?" the widow asked anxiously.

Krag showed her his revolver.

"They say he's a very good shot, that one."

Krag smiled.

"He shall not have an opportunity to demonstrate that skill," he replied.

They had barely been waiting five minutes when they

heard footfalls on the doorstep.

The detective crept behind the curtains, revolver in hand.

The widow opened the door. Through a gap in the curtains, Krag saw that it was the man in the hunting jacket. He caught a glimpse of a brutal red-bearded face.

"Is that you, Jimmy?" he heard the widow say. "I didn't expect you so early. You said you would come at midnight."

The red-bearded man muttered some incomprehensible words and slung his hunting bag on the table.

"I've come to get a straight answer from you," he said. "Are you coming with me or not?"

"But when are you leaving, Jimmy?"

"As soon as possible. My work here is done."

"Your work?"

"Yes. My work—which is no business of yours at all by the way. So: will you give me an answer?"

"What if I say no?"

"You won't. You wouldn't dare."

"But what if I do anyway?"

"Be reasonable. You know I'll cause a scandal if you do. I'll wake up the whole household and tell everybody what we got up to together. I'm sure you remember that lovely July day in Monte Carlo."

"I still don't want to go with you."

The red-bearded man grabbed her firmly by the wrist and she gave a little shriek.

In that very instant, Asbjørn Krag appeared and Jimmy

leapt aside with a curse.

"That damned spy!" he shouted, reaching for his pocket.

"Hello," Krag said in a cheery voice, moving closer to him. "As you see, I drew this little device before you had a chance to. I can assure you that both barrels are loaded."

"What the devil is the meaning of this?"

"The meaning of this," Krag replied, "is that if you do not remain perfectly still, absolutely still, I shall shoot you."

"Shoot me?"

"Yes. Just as precisely and cold-bloodedly as you shot old Aakerholm, you murderer!"

The red-bearded man sank into a chair, a livid pallor sweeping over his face.

"What do you want from me?" he asked.

"You will find out soon enough. Be so good as to close the door, Mrs Hjelm. I do not wish to be disturbed while I am speaking to this man."

CHAPTER 11

JIM CHARTER THE BOXER

J im realised by now that the detective was in deadly earnest, so he sat there fairly quietly. But his gaze flitted here and there around the room, as if seeking an escape route. A sinister vengeful glint shone in his eyes. He's like a wound-up spring, Krag thought. If I let up the pressure for so much as a second, he'll make a dash straight at me. All the while the detective was talking, he kept his revolver aimed at the other man's temple.

"You'll pay for this," hissed Jim. "I'll hand myself over the police."

"Ah, yes. Mrs Hjelm?" Krag said. "Would you be so kind as to take out the paper you will find in my coat pocket. The brown envelope."

Mrs Hjelm, who was extremely agitated and trembling like a leaf, took the envelope out of Krag's pocket."

"Hand it to Mr Charter, please," the detective said.

Jim took the letter curiously and opened it.

"Damn!" he shouted. "So you're not a doctor?"

"No. The document tells you what I am: a policeman, a detective. So if you are planning to hand yourself over to the police, you might just as well hand yourself over to me."

Jim Charter laughed and threw the envelope and letter on the table.

"What is all this? What do you want from me? Stop wasting my time and give me a quick explanation."

"I want you to confess."

"What am I supposed to be confessing to?"

"The murder of old Aakerholm."

"I do believe you're crazy," he said. "The old fool shot himself."

"No. You shot him."

"Me? Well, let's say I *did* shoot him. Even if it is true, I can prove that it was a case of self-defence, by God! He fired at me first."

"Why?"

"I'm not obliged to tell you that."

"Do you, Jim Charter, know that Aakerholm was afraid of you?"

"Yes, I do."

"Do you also know why he was afraid of you?"

"Well, I understand why now. But you'd best ask my brother about all that."

As he spoke these words, Jim looked triumphantly at the detective, as if to say: At last I've managed to surprise you. But Krag continued, quite calmly:

"I see. So Bengt is your brother then."

"Surely you couldn't have expected that?" Jim said.

"Ah, but I did."

"But can't you see how stupid you've been? How do you expect to prove that I'm Aakerholm's murderer? There isn't a jury in the world that would dare convict me."

"We already have half a confession from you."

At that, Jim laughed out loud.

"Ha ha—call that a confession? I was just having some fun at your expense."

"But we have a witness to our conversation."

"Widow Hjelm? She's as silent as the grave." Jim sent her a sharp look and added, "She wouldn't dare say a word."

The widow didn't answer, but sat still, staring at the pair of them with tearstained eyes. Her face was contorted with fear.

"But I have other proof against you," said Krag. "Just wait until you find yourself in the witness box—it will be amusing see how much courage you have then."

"The witness box! What an ass you are. Who's going to send me there?"

"I am."

"Now you're being totally ridiculous. Do you plan to arrest me all by yourself?"

"All by myself."

"But don't you see that the only thing stopping me from leaving is that little gun you're holding. I guess you're planning to put handcuffs on me with one hand while you hold the revolver in the other. Do you really think you'll get away with that? The second you get anywhere near me, I'll knock you senseless. I'm three times as strong as you are."

"You know," Krag said, "just a few minutes away at Kvamberg a clever young deputy police inspector and two sturdy constables are on guard, not to mention my friend the doctor. When I ask Widow Hjelm to go outside with my other revolver, which is in my coat, and fire two shots in the air, my friends will come running. And then you'll be trapped."

Jim wrinkled his brow.

"Well, go ahead and do it," he said. "See how that turns out—though I must say you're smarter than I gave you credit for."

"However," Asbjørn Krag continued, unmoved, "that course of action would attract too much attention. I might, for example, risk rousing the suspicions of my good friend Bengt, your talented brother. So I will carry out your arrest in another, simpler way."

He got up and approached Jim, revolver still raised.

Jim clenched his fists—two enormous hairy fists.

"Yes, yes—it's perfectly obvious that you're strong as an ox," Krag said, still calm. He spoke in a light, conversational tone that contrasted strangely with the other man's gruff outbursts.

"Maybe you're a boxer too," he continued.

"Boxer," hissed Jim. "I've knocked out men twice my size in America, so you'd better watch out."

Krag was now right next to him and could see how Jim's hairy fists clenched, white-knuckled and quivering. One blow from a fist like that could stun a bull. But Krag was still perfectly calm. He held the revolver in his left hand.

"Well I never," he said. "So you've beaten American giants to a pulp? I must say, I'd almost be inclined to risk a few thousand dollars on you myself."

He measured Jim from top to toe with an expert eye, the way a sports-loving English aristocrat examines the opponents before the match.

"Tremendous strength," he murmured.

The other man became a bit confused by this peculiar behaviour—just as Krag had expected. He continued.

"Tremendous strength, a big powerful chest, considerable endurance. But as far as I can see, you lack speed. What's more, you haven't been paying close enough attention to the latest developments in the art of boxing, which has now learned the importance of exploiting anatomy. Well, well—your choice."

Quick as a flash, Krag drove his right wrist in beneath the other man's jaw—one of the most sensitive spots on the human body. The blow stunned Jim. A greyish pallor washed over his face, blood trickled from his mouth and he crashed to the floor, smashing an etagere as he fell.

Krag paid no attention to the widow's hysterical screams. He took out some handcuffs and within two seconds they were secured around Jim's wrists. After that, he moistened his handkerchief with the contents of a small vial in his waistcoat pocket. It was chloroform. He placed the handkerchief close to Jim Charter's nose.

"Now you'll be harmless for an hour at least," he

muttered.

The widow looked at him with terrified eyes.

"Is he dead?" she asked.

"No," Krag answered with a smile. "He is just sleeping. He's had a hard day's work, poor wretch."

"Oh God—what will people say?"

"Calm yourself, dear lady," the detective said. He had already put on his hat and coat. "No one will learn what has happened here. We will fetch this fellow within the hour, and you may set your mind at rest on his account: He is floating in the land of dreams."

When Asbjørn Krag returned to Kvamberg, he noticed that the lights were still lit in Bengt's rooms. The deputy police inspector and the doctor were awaiting him impatiently.

The doctor asked if he had apprehended the mysterious stranger.

"Yes," Krag replied. "I have apprehended him. He is now lying unconscious in the Silken Girl's apartments. He is old Aakerholm's murderer, his name is Jim Charter and he is Bengt's brother."

Krag gave a short account of events at the widow's villa, then advised them on how to proceed. He and the deputy police inspector would arrest Bengt, who still appeared to be sitting up working. In the meantime, the doctor would accompany the two constables into the grounds and search the old summer house Asbjørn Krag had seen Jim Charter enter.

Just as Krag had foreseen, Bengt was sitting up writing. When the deputy police inspector entered the room, he tried to make a dash at "Doctor" Krag. But the deputy police inspector restrained him as Krag revealed his true identity: Detective Asbjørn Krag of Kristiania.

Bengt asked what they wanted and when the deputy police inspector arrested him as an accomplice in his brother Jim Charter's murder of old Aakerholm, he was so surprised that he gave himself up straight away. The policeman was able to clap him in handcuffs without a struggle. Krag and the deputy police inspector waited a few minutes for the doctor and constables to return.

"Look what we found," the doctor cried from the doorway. The constables were carrying various items of clothing, which Krag examined one by one. They were odd garments: old leather breeches, a gold-digger's belt, a brightly coloured neckerchief, a leather waistcoat, coarsely made high boots and so on.

"I thought as much," Krag muttered. "If I'd known he had his arsenal there, the drama would have been cleared up straight away and old Aakerholm's life might perhaps have been saved."

Before Bengt was taken away by the police, Krag had a brief conversation with him in private. When the conversation was over, the detective said to the deputy police inspector: "Everything is in order. Take Bengt away and drive up to the Silken Girl's house to pick up the boxer who's lying there. It'll be an easy enough job because he won't come around until he is well and truly under arrest."

A mere quarter of an hour later, Bengt drove out through the gates of Kvamberg in his own closed carriage, accompanied by the deputy police inspector and the two constables.

CHAPTER 12

THE SECRET

"You want to know the secret of the three rooms? I see that events have failed to reveal it to you. Well, that is only to be expected—you laymen have an infernal capacity to see the inexplicable and the mysterious in the most everyday phenomena. It is true enough that the so-called secret of the three rooms was the origin of this tragic drama. But the secret itself is really exceedingly mundane and ordinary. It is a trifle that becomes mysterious only because we have a habit of overlooking trifles. And this is just where the clever, cold-blooded detective must look, my dear doctor—uninfluenced by imagination and external circumstances. The minute I heard about Aakerholm's peculiar behaviour, the way he shut himself into the innermost of three chambers and refused admittance to anyone else, it was clear to me why he did it."

"Why did he, then?"

"Wait a moment, my dear doctor. In order for you to understand the entire business, I will present the case to you in sequence. This will also give you a chance to display your mental acuity, for perhaps when you hear how it all fits together, you may guess the answer before I tell you.

"Well, then, dear friend, was it not peculiar that old Aakerholm—who viewed his adopted son with utter antipathy, not to say loathing—kept him nonetheless?"

"Truth be told, I hadn't given the matter any thought."

"But you ought to have. Aakerholm adopted Bengt when he was eighteen or nineteen years old. There is no reason to believe that he found Bengt any more likeable then than now. So why did he adopt him? Bengt was an orphan but is entirely unrelated to Aakerholm, so there must have been a particular reason for it. I thought at once that this adoption could not have been an act of mercy or the manifestation of an excessive sense of duty. Only one other possibility remained: Aakerholm was rich and had decided to take this young man as his son because he wanted to make amends for something—for example a crime against Bengt's father."

"Well," said the doctor, "when you put it like that, it seems pretty obvious that this must have been the case."

"I thought so at once," Krag continued. "And I have since had it confirmed in various ways—and found out for certain this evening. If I consider Bengt a murderer—as indeed I must, since he was Jim Charter's accomplice—that means this case involved three murderers in all."

"What did you say? Three murderers?"

"That's right: Bengt, Jim Charter and old Aakerholm. For this was the dread secret that haunted the old gentleman. While he was digging for gold in California, he shot

Jim and Bengt's father in a mine. This was the crime he wished to atone for by adopting the son. Neither Bengt nor Jim had any knowledge of the old man's crime over all these years, until Bengt discovered the truth by chance three or four months ago. And that sealed the old man's fate, for he fell into the hands of two of the most cunning scoundrels I have met in my entire life.

"When Bengt learned the secret, he sent word to his brother—who was then apparently frequenting some casino or another. They decided together to torment the old man to death in order to come into possession of his wealth. But they would have to be quick, for of course his marriage to Widow Hjelm, the Silken Girl, was imminent. So they hatched a devilish plan. Aakerholm remained blissfully unaware that they knew his secret. One fine day as he was walking in his grounds, he suddenly saw before him none other than his old friend Charter, whom he had shot years ago in a California goldmine. You'll still remember how terrified he was when he returned from that walk: pale, agitated, and miserable. He even said: 'Is he a devil or a man!'"

The doctor nodded.

"Yes, I remember that," he said. "Go on."

"Jim Charter was the spitting image of his father," the detective continued. "The same muscular strength, the same red beard. Just the other day, Jim told Widow Hjelm that his appearance was worth a great deal of money. It is perfectly clear what he meant. On top of that, he dressed up in in the clothing a gold-digger would typically have worn back then."

"The arsenal in the summerhouse," murmured the doctor.

"Precisely. The old man now went from one terror to the next. They contrived to scrape a square of mercury off the back of the big mirror in the salon and one evening Aakerholm saw a threatening inscription there. I imagine it was something along the lines of "Murderer" or the like. Of course, he smashed the mirror at once. On the very same afternoon that we came down here from Kristiania, he saw the gold-digger once again, and this time, the red-headed man escaped into the pavilion in the garden; he was rescued from there, incidentally, by Bengt, who carried him over the snow. The following evening, while we were in his company, he received a secret hint to read a particular page in a particular book. Seizing the book, he leafed through to page 248, where he discovered the following sentence: 'Take that, you devil'. When, half an hour later, Bengt and I were driven to the club, he went out to meet the Silken Girl. Once again, he saw the man appear, this time in the avenue—and you know what happened after that."

"Yes," said the doctor. "All this is perfectly clear, but I still don't understand the secret of the three rooms."

The detective smiled indulgently. "Ah, I was sure you would have guessed it by now," he said. "I suppose I shall have to help you out. As you can imagine, Bengt also wondered why the old man behaved in this strange way, locking himself into the three rooms. For a long time, he left the old man to his secret, but in the end he decided to see if he could get to the bottom of it. He covertly moved aside some planks in the loft, which had a double floor. Then by laying his ear to the floor and peering in through a tiny crack, he could hear and see everything that went on. That was when he discovered the secret. Quiet now, Doctor: you still won't be able to solve this, so I must tell you everything. Bear in mind that, especially with Bengt constantly in his sight, Aakerholm's thoughts must constantly have revolved around the crime he had committed in California. In the end, the event became so firmly lodged in his imagination that he could not even shake it off when he slept. There was one episode in particular that he could never forget—the instant when he had fired a bullet into old Charter's brain, with a cry of 'Take that, you devil!' We criminologists know of many criminals who have been unmasked in the same way as Aakerholm. My dear Doctor, from the very first moment, it was clear to me that old Aakerholm talked in his sleep."

The doctor leapt up, gazing open-mouthed at the detective.

"What a fool I've been," he said, sitting down again despondently.

The detective laughed heartily.

Shortly afterwards, the doctor said, "But now at least everything is fine. And these past few days really have been exciting and fascinating for me."

"This was the tale of a fine old gentleman who was not permitted to make amends for his crime in peace," said Krag, "but was struck down by the hand of vengeance: abruptly, gruesomely, unexpectedly—the way vengeance always strikes."

"But it was also the tale of a clever detective," the doctor cried, beaming. "The greatest policeman in the entire kingdom."

"Ah, no," Krag replied—and this time he was serious, more serious than the doctor could ever recall having seen him. "It was merely the tale of an insignificant person who wasn't even capable of saving another person's life."

Two days later, Bengt and Jim both escaped from the fat police chief's jail.

Within a year, Jim became involved in a nasty train robbery in America. He was caught, convicted, and sent to the electric chair.

Of Bengt, Asbjørn Krag has neither seen nor heard anything since. But he has the distinct feeling that he will meet him again some day, perhaps in some shadowy stairway or on some desolate road.

THE END

A Note
From The Publisher

Through Three Rooms has finally made its way into an English translation more than a hundred years after its initial publication - but we think you'll agree it's worth the wait! If you enjoyed it, don't forget to check out our other Asbjørn Krag books and the other books in the Scandinavian Mystery Classics series.

Kabaty Press is a micro-press with a mission to bring undiscovered and untranslated gems to your bookshelves. You can find us on www.kabatypress.com - why not sign up to our mailing list while you are there, and make sure you don't miss out on any of our new releases?

The Scandinavian Mystery Classics Series

THE MAN WHO PLUNDERED THE CITY: AN ASBJØRN KRAG MYSTERY

Sven Elvestad
(trans. Frederick H Martens)

When a series of jewel thefts scandalise Christiania (now Oslo), detective Asbjørn Krag encounters a master criminal who has his measure–or does he? From the dark brickyards on the city's outskirts to the bright lights of the Grand Hotel, Krag must use all his skill to turn the tables on the gang and their mysterious leader.

BEWARE OF RAILWAY-JOURNEYS: A SCANDINAVIAN MYSTERY CLASSIC

Frank Heller
(trans. Robert Emmons Lee)

When Allan Kragh impulsively follows a beautiful grey-eyed woman onto a train, he finds himself sharing a hotel with the Maharajah of Nasirabad and his fabled jewel collection. . . and a master criminal intent on stealing it.

THE GRAND DUKE'S LAST CHANCE

Frank Heller
(trans. Robert Emmons Lee)

The Grand Dukes of the tiny island of Minorca have been happily bankrupt for generations. But when the current Grand Duke is threatened by blackmail, and a band of revolutionaries takes over the island in his absence, the situation looks bleak – until he crosses paths with Mr Collin and a mysterious woman under his protection.

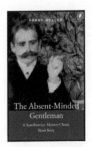

THE ABSENT-MINDED GENTLEMAN: A SCANDINAVIAN MYSTERY CLASSIC SHORT STORY

Frank Heller
(trans. Robert Emmons Lee)

When a counterfeiting ring rocks London, the trail leads to a curiosity shop and a professor offering a treatment for 'absent-minded gentlemen'–but can Detective Kenyon get to the bottom of the clever scheme?

Lightning Source UK Ltd.
Milton Keynes UK
UKHW011826240223
417611UK00004B/182